ACKNOWLEDGEMENTS

I acknowledge my late parents Henry and Sandra Wilson for instilling a strong work ethic and love and support for me and my family. Mom you would always joke saying "I could write a book." Well, I hope you enjoy mine.

To my wife Mary Ann thank you for your patience for putting up with me through these years. Your published works eleven years ago were an inspiration for this work.

To my wonderful children Kaitlyn, Kevin and Michael, I am proud of each of you as you have become successful and caring adults. I am excited to be a part of your future successes.

To my mother-in law Luz, thank you for renewing my faith and being a positive influence.

Rick and Justine thank you for reading the rewritten manuscripts and providing encouragement throughout the writing process.

Kevin, David, John, Jim, Rusty, Mike and Peter, thank you for your calls which distracted me from my creative writing block and being there.

Sully's Squad would not have been possible without a chance meeting with author Heath Lee. Your question is etched in mind. "Everyone has a story, what's yours?"

Abigail Santamaria whose tireless editing and guidance was not only enlightening but provided a strong foundation for future writing. I remember when you told me I had to rewrite the first draft and start again. You talked me through it and I am grateful.

My appreciation to Meradith Kill of The Troy Book Makers whose valuable recommendations for cover design and layout transformed a bunch of words into a reality.

LOOSE LIPS
MIGHT
Sink Ships

THIS POSTER IS PUBLISHED BY THE HOUSE OF SEAGRAM AS PART OF ITS CONTRIBUTION TO THE NATIONAL VICTORY EFFORT.

REMINDERS
of a world prior to mobile technology

A soldier's available time was restricted while in training. Despite this there was still an expectation from many families to regularly write home. Communication was in the form of writing a letter, not texts, Twitter, Facebook messenger, FaceTime or cell phone. Letters could take weeks or months to be delivered.

Letters were subject to censorship reviews. When time allowed soldiers could use approved templates. The format provided a number of phrases to communicate how you were doing. Limited writing space allowed for a brief greeting. Although most soldiers were ignorant as to the details of military plans, this was considered a necessary precaution, in order to prevent leaked information. The following are personal examples of actual templates.

The following posters "Loose Lips might Sinks Ships" and "He's Watching You" are reminiscent of that period. As already noted, a soldier had to be careful of communicating anything related to their military training. On the home front, citizens were expected to remain cautious, an enemy spy could be within listening distance. Today this level of anxiety and consternation would be labeled paranoia. However, this was just one example of daily life during World War II. Every American in combat or home had to work together to defeat the enemy.

Sully sends a brief note home to his mother Laura and his brother and sisters while in training in 1941

TOP: *Sully writes a brief note and Mother's Day card template to his mother Laura in 1943 just after North African campaign and prior to Sicily*

BOTTOM: *Mother's Day card template from Sully to his mother Laura during training in 1942*

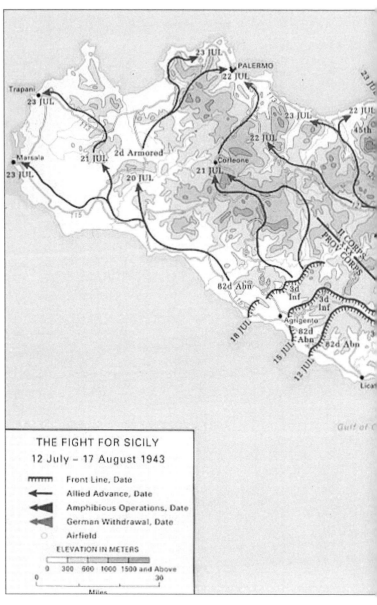

Sully's Squad would have followed a path similar to the 1st Division.

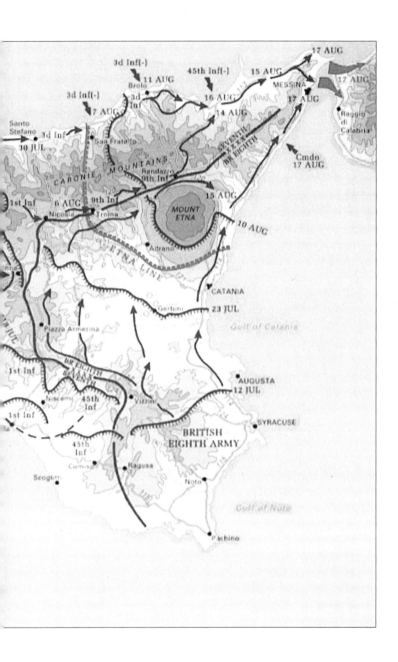

CHAPTER 1

In the dark of midnight, massive guns fire simultaneously on the Sicilian shore. For a split second after each explosion, yellow and orange light reveals the deck of our boat, flashing glimpses of hundreds of soldiers as we wait in anticipation.

The next blast is closer, louder. It doesn't just light up the deck. It flings me on my side like I'm one of the tin soldiers I used to play with as a kid. As I roll, I can see Coney on his knees, searching for his helmet.

Then the night goes black again.

My legs shake as I stagger upright. It's 1:30am on July 10, 1943. For the past several hours we've traveled through a gale, rough seas tossing our three-story vessel like a child with a ball. The wind blows the rain in sideways, straight at you, stinging the body. I've been soaked for hours, and I'm shaking uncontrollably now from the chill.

I press my palms against my ears, trying to block the sound as I stare out at the shells bursting on the distant shore. The tracks of the explosives tracing through the sky look like falling stars and meteors heading for earth. I'm in awe, but I'm also afraid.

As the deck bucks under me, I reach into my pocket and pull out a small velvet pouch. I untie the drawstring, open the top, and hold it under my nose to inhale the sweet scent of home. My mother. Lilacs from our backyard on a summer evening. Just over a year ago, as I boarded the bus for basic training, my mother had pressed the pouch into the palm of my hand. "Remember," she'd said, wrapping her arms around me in a final hug. "Home will always be with you." When I found my seat on the bus, I stretched open the pouch and immediately smelled lilacs. The little sac was packed with fresh petals; though they disintegrated with time, their scent had not. My mother knew I would need her words and the comforting smell of home.

"Keep in line!" yells one of the sergeants.

I glance around, looking for Coney. I'd given him the two packs of cigarettes they'd issued us a couple days ago because I don't smoke unless I'm scared. But, right now, I'm desperate for a smoke.

I catch Coney's eye and put two fingers up to my mouth. He nods and hands me a cigarette. I lean over for a light, then cough as I inhale.

Our line moves forward. The men in front drop over the ropes into the waiting assault craft. Every moment, I'm steps closer to climbing over the side myself. The sound becomes deafening. The boat pitches so I stumble from side to side, and now I can see my fingers shaking in the glow from the cigarette. The smell of gunpowder and the cigarette smoke scratch my throat. I spit, then cough. But the choking air up here is still better than the stench below deck, where vomit slicks the floors and the smell of shit from backed up toilets mingles with the body odor from hundreds of sweating soldiers.

"Gather around!" Sargent Spinelli yells, trying to keep our unit tight. "We're moving closer to the ropes."

All around us, other officers shout to keep the line from holding up. "Let's go boys! Form two lines! Keep moving!"

Coney punches me on the shoulder, a signal to move. I nod and flick my cigarette towards the churning water below.

Fear and confidence war within me as I gaze toward the shore. *How can the enemy survive these guns?* I wonder. Suddenly, Lucky falls against me. I catch him before he tumbles to the deck.

"Lucky! Lucky!" I yell, slapping his face.

"Get some water!" Coney shouts.

Hank beats me to it, unscrewing his canteen and splashing Lucky's face. Lucky's eyes spring open and he stands up on his own two feet again. Our squad shuffles forward until Sargent Spinelli stands at the rope, looking down at the dark ocean. We're up. I try to get Sargent's attention to tell him that Lucky isn't doing well. But the darkness and noise makes it impossible to communicate with anyone more than a foot away, and Sargent is a good twenty feet ahead.

But Doc is near enough to catch my meaning, and he comes over to investigate the situation. After a quick back and forth with Lucky, Doc nods to me, indicating that Lucky's okay. Everyone on the boat is anxious, seasick and weak, I realize, just like Lucky. But this is Lucky's first time seeing action, so his nerves are no doubt even more on edge than mine.

I pat him on the back as he looks me in the eye, letting me know he's okay. I lift two fingers to my eyes and point towards the ropes, signaling him to focus on the task before us. He nods and turns to look straight ahead.

I take a deep breath and look back towards the shore. Our training was thorough, but there's still no real way to prepare yourself for an actual descent with wind, rain, and sea spray slicking the ropes. Sargent Spinelli, known by the squad as Sully, turns toward us, his face illuminated by flashes from the shells exploding on shore. He touches his helmet, backpack and weapon, signaling us to check that our gear is strapped and secured.

We're in two lines, ready to climb down in pairs. I'm going to be in the third pair with Lucky, and since I'm the senior soldier of the two of us, I feel responsible for taking him into action. "You can do this!" I yell, punching him in the arm, gesturing for him to look ahead. He nods, his gaze fixed forward. Another shell explosion lights up the night. I see that his eyes are filled with fear. I know that look. I've seen it in other soldiers. And I've felt it myself.

I look down at the landing craft, rocking forcefully below. I can hear the faint sound of its engine below the naval gunfire. Our own ship continues to rock. My stomach starts to churn like the angry sea below.

How the hell are we going to land in this weather? I hope the Germans will think no one's stupid enough to invade tonight. But I'm afraid they may know better.

Then, suddenly, there are no more men between Lucky and me and the sea. It's our turn to board the assault vessel.

I prepare to climb down the ropes by grabbing the top of the deck.

"Lucky, you with me?"

He nods.

"Let me hear you say it!" I yell.

"I'm with you!"

I place my left leg over the rail and the straps from my eighty-pound pack cut into my shoulders like knives. The pain is a surprise. *Dammit.*

I look down at the landing craft while holding onto the ropes with my hands and feet. Then I turn to my left to check on Lucky. *Good.* He's moving in sequence with me.

Below, Willy and Hank are ready to release into the craft. I'm relieved for them; between them, they're carrying a bazooka and dozens of pounds of ammunition. I descend the ropes slow and steady, one step at a time, cautiously alternating a leg and the opposite arm in sequence down the cold, slippery ropes.

We're now about half way down. The destroyers on either side of us choose this moment to fire in unison, and the rope responds by swinging violently.

I'm smashed into the side of our boat. My body spins, but I hold tight to the wet ropes. Below, I still see the craft bouncing. But when I look to my left, Lucky's gone.

Where the hell did he go?

There's no more time to look. The rope steadies, and I continue my downward climb. Above me, Romeo and Marty climb over the ship's side loaded with a machine gun and ammunition.

I'm close enough to the assault craft to release my grip and drop. But when I do, a large wave slams the assault craft so hard that the hull rises to smack my nose. A gush of warm blood fills my nostrils and I cry out in pain.

Unbelievable! I fought in the North Africa campaign without a scratch. In all my years as a baseball catcher, I never hurt my nose. But now I'm not even back in combat yet and my nose is bleeding. Still, it's not the kind of injury that's important at a moment like this. I need to keep it to myself.

And I need to find Lucky. Each time a shell explodes on shore, I scan the boat, but I don't see him.

"Move to the back, mates," yells the coxswain, struggling to keep the craft steady.

A searchlight from the ship shines into the grey-green sea near the craft. Beyond is so much darkness. And then even the searchlight goes off.

As I look around for the squad, a wave of sea water rushes into the landing craft and pelts my face. The rocking of the craft forces me to sink to my knees, clinging to the side. When I turn my head to get my bearings, I see Sully next to me.

"Where's Lucky?" I shout. Seawater splashes into my open mouth. "He was next to me and now he's gone!"

A flash from a naval gun illuminates Sully's face. His expression tells me not to question him. "Arty, sit and focus on our mission! He'll show up." Then Sully turns toward the rest of the squad, who I now see are gathered all around us. "Keep your focus, everyone!"

I've seen death before. I spent six months in the campaign in North Africa, which left a path of death and destruction. I still remember the first German I killed. I never saw his face, but he dropped from my rifle shot and didn't move. I remember the first camel I ever saw lying dead in the desert, with vultures devouring his flesh. But what I remember most are the smells. Decaying and burning flesh creates a ghastly stench that attaches to your hair, clothes and memory. But even if you've seen combat before, it's not something you get used to.

"Keep your position. No quick moves! We don't want to rock the vessel anymore," the coxswain yells.

Sully goes on giving us our orders. "Keep your weapons and ammo dry. Throw up on your boots."

We're standing side by side, bouncing into each other and the boat. My boots are soaking in a mixture of seawater and vomit. Blood drips from my nose.

"Arty, look me in the eye," Sully yells. "Are you with me?"

I nod.

"Say it!" Sully orders. His sharp tone snaps me into focus. This is a matter of life and death.

"Yes, Sargent, I'm ready!" Responding out loud increases my confidence. Sully has a gift for knowing how and when to take a soldier aside. I'd seen him do it in North Africa, with Hank.

Hank's full name was Henrik Klausen, and he'd been born in Germany to Jewish parents. But as his homeland slid into fascism, they'd been forced to flee for America. When we rounded up German prisoners in North Africa, Hank glared at each one as they walked past him. Then he started yelling.

"Who's from Munich? Anyone from Munich?"

He was searching for anyone who might give him information about his German family and the friends who had been ripped out of his life when his family fled into exile. But he was also freaking out.

"Hank," Sully had said, firmly. "Over here." He motioned to a patch of shade under a palm tree. Since several of us had already crowded into the welcome shade, I was close enough to hear their conversation.

"Hank, you're an excellent soldier. You work well with Willy and your instincts are some of the best in the squad," Sully began. "I don't know what you're feeling. I wasn't born German. I wasn't forced away from my home. But I need you to be there for the squad. For yourself, too. If you're distracted by the dead and by the captured, then you'll soon be among the dead and captured yourself. You understand?"

"Yes, Sargent."

"I'm sure eventually we'll be in Italy," Sully told him. "That's where my parents came from."

I knew from talking with Sully that he'd been born Salvatore Spinelli. His parents had immigrated to the U.S., where his name was changed to Sullivan. They ended up in Granville, New York, the colored slate capital of the world, an hour from where I grew up. His father had worked a slate quarry and served in the army in the Great War, just like Sully was serving now. We'd discovered that both our mothers grew large vegetable gardens. And, like me, Sully was the oldest child in his family.

"In Italy," Sully had gone on, still talking with Hank, "I'll need to keep my focus. Maybe you can remind me, ok?"

Hank nodded. "Yes," he said. "I can do that."

But we're far from the heat of the North African desert now, bobbing in the black water off this new coast. And for the first time, enemy searchlights on the coastal defenses start to shine onto the beach landing zones. As those searchlights paint the targets, enemy cruisers and destroyers turn their attention to them. German anti-aircraft guns are strafing American paratroopers as they attempt to land. I feel bad for those guys. Trying to land in this wind and rain is bad enough without taking enemy fire. But I'm also relieved to know we'll have them on our side when we land ourselves. That is, if we all make it to the beach alive.

As we circle the ship, keeping in line with other craft getting in position to make the beach landing, waves hit the craft's side, muffling the sound of the engine. Most heads are down. I hear someone puke, but I can't tell who. I worry the boat might flip and we'll all drown before we get to take a shot. Right now, our enemy is the angry green sea, doing its best to keep us from even making it to land.

Sully turns back to us. "When you jump, stay low. If you fall, get up and keep moving onto the beach. We're a team. Danny Boy, Marty, Kelly, Wolcott—follow the experienced guys. Willy, Coney, Hank, Romeo, Doc, Arty—guide the new guys. Work together."

I notice Sully doesn't mention Lucky's name, but there's no time to dwell on the omission.

The coxswain interrupts. "Okay mates, we're heading towards shore. Prepare for an even bumpier ride. And may God be with you."

My stomach's in knots and at times my nerves overcome rational thoughts. I can't stop wondering about Lucky. But the sights and smells of death in North Africa also flash in my mind, without my permission.

Large shells are being fired over our heads onto the shore. *Please don't misfire*, I plead silently as I watch them trace through the sky towards the beach. *Kaboom! Kaboom!* More shells, their sound blunted somewhat by the pounding waves.

I spit towards my boots, blood and saliva. The bleeding from my nose seems to have slowed. As I look back towards the shore, my gut churning with each explosion, I realize that my present discomfort may be the best I'll feel for a while. When our boots hit that sand, we'll be fighting for our lives as well as for our country.

I glance over at Coney and we make eye contact. Hard to believe that just yesterday, he and I were playing baseball on the ship's deck off the North African coast. I pretend to pitch him a ball. He plays along, pretending to catch it.

CHAPTER 2

My mind drifts back to that game the day before. As usual, I'd been playing catcher while Coney pitched.

"Ugh," I grunted, as a fast ball from Coney stung my left hand.

"Ball two!" yelled Doc Ito.

"What're you looking at, Doc?" barked Coney. He stepped back on the makeshift mound, planting both feet in a stance worthy of his title as an All-Star pitcher for his Edison, New Jersey, high school team. The North African sun shone on his short blond hair. Leaning forward, he stared into my glove with the command of a major league pitcher, though he had only recently turned 18.

Coney, also known as Michael Cohen, is my best friend. He's the youngest of four children from a blue collar Jewish family. He stands an inch taller than my five foot 10 frame and he's grown stronger since our first meeting in the Grand Central Station Bus Terminal.

Both of us were on our way to Fort Benning, Georgia, for basic training. Sitting together on the bus out of New York City, we talked for hours about our high school careers, bonded over our shared love of baseball, and dreamed about how after the war we would both play in the major leagues. We pounded our hands into our glove pockets as we looked onto the busy streets. And when we got off the bus in Washington, DC, we were fast friends.

Squatting in my catcher's position, I flashed my right index finger. Coney shook off the initial sign. I returned with two fingers and he nodded. I rose from my position like I had just a year earlier as an All-Star catcher from Saratoga Springs. I was just 15 years old then. A lifetime ago.

Coney stepped back on his left foot, with his arms in a triangle position above his head. Then he pivoted on his right leg and lunged forward, leaving his left hand, arm and shoulder to follow. I watched the ball leave his hand, spinning and dropping towards my glove. *Smack*.

"Ball three! Three balls and two strikes," shouts a grinning Doc Ito.

Doc, also known as Akio Ito, is the squad medic. A native of Hawaii, he enlisted out of high school three years ago with the dream of someday becoming a doctor. In North Africa, he was fearless. On one especially fierce day of fighting, two squad brothers, Jazz and Country Boy, were both injured by shrapnel from German Artillery. Doc and I saw them lying wounded within the line of fire of a German machine gun nest armed by four men. I threw three grenades and killed two of the four, but not the gunner. But despite my warning, Doc ran into the line of fire to treat our guys. Because of him, we were able to carry them out. And they're recovering today.

Coney bent over, holding his left pitching arm while glaring at Doc Ito. As his white tank top shifted, the shrapnel scar on his left shoulder seemed to glow. He pounded his left hand into the glove several times, mumbling under his breath. He stepped back onto the mound and I put down my right index finger again for a fastball. With a determined look, he nodded, wound up and released his fastest pitch yet. It hit with an even harder *smack* than the last.

"Strike three!" Doc Ito yelled, raising his right hand as he danced a jig. "You're out of here!"

But while Coney and I were still high-fiving our victory over the unlucky batter, Sully had appeared on deck.

"Gather around," he called to us, gesturing toward a shady area on the top deck.

I stared out at the North African coastline, wishing it were North America. Wishing I could be home playing baseball on a real field instead of on a ship headed for battle.

Sully handed each of us a small booklet. The front of the booklet said S-I-C-I-L-Y. I'd never seen the word.

"This is where we're headed," Sully said, holding up his copy. "The island of Sicily. Read the booklet. Familiarize yourself with the geography and language, especially common phrases—they'll come in handy. Memorize as much as you can."

"Any information on the German divisions?" asked Hank.

"Why?" Coney asked sarcastically. "Are you looking for old Nazi school friends?"

Hank stormed over to face Coney. I moved in, prepared to break up a fight. Sully stood by silently, allowing the guys space to work it out themselves.

"Coney," Hank said, sharply, "you're Jewish. You were born in America. You have no idea. Every night, we didn't know if we'd be woken up by Nazis. My father would come home and lock the front door. My mother always breathed a sigh of relief that he was home. But one night a mob came. They burned our home and everything we owned. With God's help, we escaped and arrived in America. I love America and that's why I fight. But Germany is still my home, too." Hank shook his head at Coney and stepped away. "You just don't fucking understand."

A minute later, Coney approached Hank with an extended hand. "I'm sorry for being an asshole," he said.

Hank's expression remained skeptical, but he shook Coney's hand.

Sully cleared his throat, reached into his pocket and pulled out a small bundle. "Mail!"

"Yeah, baby! I can't wait to read my letters from good old Beantown," Romeo exclaimed. He'd joined the squad as a replacement the last month in North Africa, and his nickname was short for his given one, Carmen Romano.

"Here you go, Romeo," said Sully. Smiling, Romeo sniffed his envelope. His girlfriend had doused it with her perfume. "Ah," he sighed, walking away.

"Arty," said Sully, handing me two letters.

They're both addressed to Arthur Murtaugh, postmarked from home. I recognize my mother's handwriting on the first envelope.

Dear Arthur,

Dad, Suzanne, Catherine and I miss you very much. We sit around the radio every night after dinner and listen to the news, trying to learn all we can about the battle in North Africa. After thirty minutes or so, your sisters usually leave— Suzanne goes to her room to read her Nancy Drew mysteries, while Catherine goes outside to check on the victory garden. Your father listens to the complete broadcast while reading the paper.

Both of your sisters miss you very much. Suzanne at times will wipe away a tear while listening to the newscasts. Catherine will come to me after listening to the big guns and give me a hug. They're both praying for you Arthur and they would love for you to write more. I know it must be hard to write while at war, but please think of them.

On weekends, your father and I go to the movies. We watch the reels at the beginning and search for you. My heart aches as I watch all you boys in harm's way. Your father stares at the screen and his eyes get shiny. He'll fake a sneeze or an itchy eye before he ever admits to crying, but I can tell that he's holding back tears.

Mrs. Smith asks about you every time I see her. She said Mr. Smith wants you to know that three calves were born last month and he listens to the newscasts nightly. The school baseball team is in first place and your friend Billy is pitching well.

High School graduation is soon and, Arthur, my heart aches. You would've graduated this year. You're always the youngest in every class. Please promise me when you come home that you'll go back to school.

There's so much I could tell you, but I don't want to start crying. The girls are asleep. Your father's dozed off in the recliner listening to Tommy Dorsey. He still works very hard. He's at the plant by 6am and has been working overtime every night. I don't think he's had a full night's sleep since you left.

My beloved son, please come home safe. We all love you very much.

Mom

I carefully slipped the letters into my pocket alongside my lilac petals pouch. It was a double-edged sword, getting letters from home. I thought all the time about how the family was doing, and I was always glad to hear from them. But it wasn't easy to know how much they worried and missed me.

As I looked around, I saw Danny Boy leaning over Lucky, who was busily sketching something, his back propped against a pile of rope on the deck. "What're you drawing?" Danny Boy asked.

"The shore line." Lucky flashed his sketch briefly without looking up. Then he flipped the paper back down quickly and continued to draw. We knew Lucky's real name was Eric Lindbergh, but other than that, we didn't know him well. He'd joined us after North Africa. He seemed jumpy, skittish. All of us wondered how he'd handle action.

"Where did you learn that?" Danny Boy asked.

"I don't know," Lucky answered. "I always liked it. My mother used to take me to art class, when I was young. I was pretty good."

"Art class?" asked Romeo.

Head down, continuing to draw, Lucky replied: "There were some art galleries in Newport that my mom would take my brother and me to. My brother's three years older. He didn't like to draw or paint. He wanted to be out playing baseball or football."

"Sounds like my kind of guy," replied Coney. "Is he in the Army, too?"

Lucky flinched, but continued to draw, staring down at the paper as if he could see right through it. "He's in the battleship Arizona at the bottom of Pearl Harbor."

I looked up at the sky. We all got quiet until Coney broke the silence. "Damn," he said softly. "Sorry, man."

"My parents didn't deserve that," Lucky said. "They never got his body back, so I don't think they ever really believed he was gone. They always hoped for a miracle." He continued drawing, pressing harder on the paper now.

"I was a senior in high school when he was killed," Lucky went on. "When I enlisted, I joined the army so I'd be fighting on solid ground. If something happens to me, at least my body will be returned home. I just want this war over so I can go to art school."

His voice was emotionless as he said this, but I could see him rocking back and forth. It made me want to cry, for all of our family members.

But Romeo had gotten something in the mail that he couldn't wait to share. "Look at the wheels on this, fellas," he shouted, holding up a picture of a red 1943 Italian sports car. "Just like me, guys—short and sleek." We all welcomed the change of subject.

"That's a sweet set of wheels," Danny Boy said, nodding.

"Danny Boy, I don't know which is brighter—your hair or the color of the car," Hank said, laughing.

"I used to drive my grandfather's 1934 Ford Deluxe Roadster all over Eastern Pennsylvania. My whole singing group could fit in it. We'd ride in luxury to our singing gigs."

Danny Boy had joined the squad as a replacement after North Africa was secured. During training he wasn't the swiftest soldier. He often coughed from the dusty desert air, and his pale skin filled with freckles from the sun. But when he sang, even Romeo stopped talking.

Sully emerged from the crowd of soldiers on the deck. "Any updated life insurance paperwork must be completed and your pack organized," he told us. "They've predicted heavy winds and rain the last half of our trip and the landings. See you below by 1600." Then he walked off, heading for the stairs that led below deck.

"Hey," Marty asked, "who took my hat?"

As he bent over to lift his pack, everyone around him could see Marty's hat, sticking out of his back pocket.

"You mean this?" Romeo asked, grabbing the hat.

Marty spun around in surprise as the rest of us burst into laughter.

"Marty," Hank said, shaking his head, "You'd forget your head if it wasn't attached." This brought another appreciative roar of laughter. Ramon Martinez, or Marty, had joined the squad after North Africa was liberated. He hadn't been around as long as some of the other guys, but his forgetfulness was already legendary in the squad.

"Marty," Coney joked, "did you lose the machine gun, too?" Coney winked at Romeo. "Romeo, better make sure that machine gun is strapped to his leg."

But just as Sully had predicted, an intense wind was starting to pick up. Cigarette butts began to blow in swirls around the decks, and we watched a guy chase all the way across the deck after his baseball cap, which had been snatched off his head by the wind. He caught it just before it plunged into the sea, and we all gave him a good cheer. But by now the clouds were spread all over the sky like grey bed sheets, and deep troughs of water had replaced the gentle waves.

Time to head below.

A large wave rocks the landing craft, knocks me into Sully, and brings me back to the present moment. As soon as I come back to myself, I almost wish I hadn't. Since we've almost arrived, closing on the beaches, the friendly naval shelling has stopped. The shelling accuracy from our side has been outstanding. All searchlights appear to be destroyed.

In the darkness on the boat, each soldier seems immersed in his own thoughts. I can just see Sully close his eyes and slowly move his lips. With his right arm, he makes the sign of the cross and blesses himself.

To my right, Coney and Hank talk quietly.

The coxswain breaks the silence: "We're one hundred meters out. Godspeed, mates! Give those bloody Nazis hell. See you in Messina!"

"Okay, take off your rifle covers," directs Sully. "Remember, watch your step and run low to the ground. If you fall, get up. Keep moving."

My heart races. I'm short of breath and sweating profusely, despite the freezing sea spray. I take several slow, deep breaths through my mouth and feel a little more calm.

Sully yells again: "When the ramp is down, get the hell out! I'll see you at the rendezvous point!"

The ramp clatters, metal on metal, while the chain system screeches as it releases. Finally, the ramp crashes into the shallow water with a great splash. Sully's Squad has arrived.

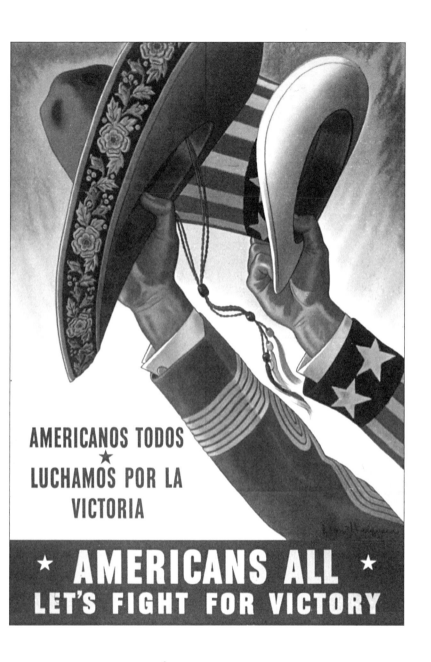

CHAPTER 3

I'm thrown forward, my helmet slipping over my eyes.

"Get out, move, move, move," yells Sully, as he stumbles out and begins to run.

When I get my footing again I hesitate, wanting someone else to go first.

"Keep moving, mates," yells the coxswain.

I slip down the ramp and begin to run, only to fall on my knees in sand after a few steps. This is my second landing. I'd forgotten how impossible it is to run in wet sand with wet boots and a loaded pack.

Darkness blankets the beach except for pockets of fires in the brush off the shoreline.

"Get out of my way, soldier!" Hank yells in my direction as I begin to put one foot in front of the other again.

Sully maintains a steady stream of orders from up ahead. "Keep moving! Pick up the pace!"

The air carries a symphony of sounds: the squish from soaked boots, the clang of metal from our packs, heavy breathing from the squad. Off to the right is the *rat, tat, tat* of enemy machine guns and *bang, bang, bang* of enemy anti-aircraft rapid bursts at allied planes. Not to mention the wind and rain tagging along, no matter how far we make it up the beach.

"Squad," Sully calls from the upper beachline. "Over here!"

I make it to the low stone wall he's taken shelter by, and squat with my back against it. Sully takes up a safe position, protected by the stone, and hands a poncho to Coney and Danny Boy. While they shield him, he kneels and pulls out a map.

For the first time I'm able to look out at the sea. To the east, the sun is below the horizon but beginning to peek through a layer of clouds and fog. The morning light reveals a massive armada of vessels with large barrage balloons flying in and out of the low overhead clouds. Hundreds of landing craft remind me of sardine cans full of soldiers approaching the beach. Each boat is being thrown about by the rising and falling of the waves. This, we've been told, is the largest amphibious invasion force in the history of war.

Taking several deep breaths, I fill my lungs with fresh air.

"Check that your weapons are loaded and watch for nervous trigger fingers. We're not looking to engage the enemy," Sully warns. "Our initial mission is to support capturing the town of Gela and to secure the beach access roads. We've landed further west from our target than planned. We need to move fast."

We scramble over the slick stone wall and begin a fast pace to the east. A layer of fog hovers around a grove of fruit trees. Their thick brown trunks, creased with deep crevices, lead to branches covered with leaves and green oval-shaped fruits slightly larger than grapes. My empty stomach pulls me in their direction. I look around cautiously to see if I can get a piece of fruit without Sully noticing, then quickly pick several pieces and pop one in my mouth. The bitter taste is surprisingly pleasant: my first taste of Sicilian olives. I spit out the pits on our way out of the grove, grabbing as many as I can for a breakfast on the run.

The torrential rain of the past several hours slows to a steady drizzle. The wind calms to a gentle breeze. Moving at a swift pace, we're flanked on either side by hundreds of other divisional infantry who all landed on the beach in the night, just like us.

Short spurts of gunfire pop ahead. The boom of artillery becomes louder with each step.

"Kelly, bring the radio," Sully calls out, without breaking his stride. Kelly hands him the radio receiver, carrying the body of the radio with him in a dark green back pack as he trails beside Sully. "Lieutenant Cook," Sully says, "Sargent Spinelli. We landed two miles west and are heading towards Gela. There's cover on our flanks. So far no enemy encounters."

Sully listens for a moment to whatever Lieutenant Cook has to say, then answers, "Ok sir," and hands the receiver back to Kelly, who secures the radio.

The fog has lifted and sun begins to shine on a countryside of rolling hills and trees. Displaced birds circle overhead, their daily routine of foraging disrupted by the 11th division. It's a sharp contrast to my most recent eight months of desert living, when sand was sometimes the only thing we could see for miles, and sweat seemed to evaporate off a man as soon as it appeared on his skin. It's hot here, too, but humidity blankets us as we troop up and down the rolling hills. The sound of breaking twigs and the squawking of sea gulls replace the squish of our wet boots.

"Arty, what do you think?" Coney asks.

When I look over, I see that somewhere, he's found a yellow flower and stuck it in his helmet band. "I'm saving it," he says with a wink, "for the first pretty girl I see."

I give him a thumbs up.

Smoke rises above the hills as we approach the sounds of combat. The fog continues to lift. The skies ahead and behind become active with air assaults on enemy positions. We're now patrolling uphill at a steep grade, high enough that I can see over the patch of olive trees where we started and the beach beyond. The clear blue-green surf rolls gently, dotted with floating bodies and overturned assault crafts.

To our east, landings continue, easier now without the wind and rain. Further out to sea, naval fire intensifies as enemy aircraft begin an attack on the armada. As we watch, German fighters dive towards the ships. Above us, one circles, getting ready to head back for a second round of terror. A black swastika against the grey metal is clearly visible on its wing.

We reach a gravel road and walk single file on either side. Ahead of me, Coney occasionally raises his left pitching arm to stretch his shoulder.

I playfully kick gravel towards his feet.

He turns and whispers, "Stop it, asshole," with a playful smirk.

Before I can kick another spray of gravel at Coney, Sully suddenly stops. "Down," he whispers. "And be quiet."

I drop and crawl on all fours into a gully. A few hundred feet ahead is an intersection with plenty of brush and large trees that might be giving cover to the enemy. Sully moves up on the right side of the road, motioning Marty and Romeo to set up their machine gun to my left.

Sully, Willy and Hank crawl ahead, towards the intersection. Their movement is shielded by the sounds of combat to the east. Sully raises his left arm and motions the rest of the squad to move in.

I crawl forward, crouched as low as possible. I'm now within one hundred feet of the intersection. The silence is broken by the sound of a truck shifting gears. To my left on the road are several trucks heading towards the intersection, sending up clouds of dust that rise above the trees.

Sully motions for us to stay down.

"What do you think?" I whisper to Coney. "We just landed. Our trucks are still on the beach."

Coney replies, "Germans, for sure. Keep low, and no nervous trigger finger. Wait for Sully's command."

I turn and pass the same message to Danny Boy.

Sully, Willy and Hank are out of sight now, ahead of us. The trucks that just passed us approach the intersection. As they do, a pair of Germans emerge from the bushes. One waves his arm, motioning the lead truck to stop. He's wearing black boots, a blue uniform and an oblong dark blue helmet.

"What's going on?" Danny Boy whispers nervously.

I put my right index finger to my lips, signaling him to be quiet.

Morning sun lights the intersection like a stage. I'm able to count at least five trucks on the road. German soldiers continue talking while the truck engines idle. Beyond the intersection, I can tell something is hidden in the thick brush. Two other Germans emerge from the brush now. I see something that looks a lot like a gun barrel sticking out of the leaves behind them.

"What's… what's taking so long?" Danny Boy stutters.

"Quiet!" I whisper through clenched teeth. But I know how he feels. Doing nothing in the face of the enemy can make even the most experienced soldier anxious. My legs start to stiffen as I slowly shift my weight away from the rocks that are digging into my ass. Sweat beads up on my forehead, then drips into my eyes and burns. A mosquito lands on my left hand and enjoys his breakfast. I brush him away silently, aware that the sound of slapping him could give away our position. He dives back for round two. I imagine I'm a navy ship and he's a German fighter: I catch him between my right index finger and thumb and crush them together. His stomach full of blood explodes on my left hand.

On the left side of the road, a few steps beyond me, a couple of fearless gulls peck at a dead rabbit. They dance around, poking at the carcass, lifting their heads to swallow pieces of flesh.

We've only been in this position for a few minutes, but it seems like hours.

The *whoosh* of a German artillery gun shakes the ground so hard it seems to even jolt the air. I stiffen. The rattle of guns in the distance is now following the boom of artillery guns. This may be the beginning of the fight for the town of Gela.

Kaboom! An explosion lights up the lead truck in the intersection. A second explosion, and the barrel sticking out of the bushes is no more. The Germans at the intersection are now human torches. With a third explosion, another truck bursts into flames. Within seconds, German soldiers, some of them on fire, jump out of the trucks.

"Enemy in the open!" yells Coney, and we all open fire.

Shots from Marty and Romeo end the misery for the human torches. Coney, who throws a grenade as accurately as he throws a baseball, sends several grenades after the escaping German infantry. Each explodes, showering enemy soldiers with shrapnel.

When I pause my firing, I realize Danny Boy's been struggling with his rifle. He hasn't fired a shot.

"Give it to me," I yell, gesturing for him to give me his gun. When he does, I unlatch the bolt and reload his ammunition. Then I lock the bolt and fire a test shot towards the Germans. When it fires, I hand the rifle back and yell, "Start firing!"

A new, even louder explosion sets the remaining trucks ablaze. The smell of gasoline fills my nostrils. As I move up into position, I'm blasted with intense heat.

My rifle is now nestled between my right shoulder and armpit as I lay on my stomach. I empty a full round in what feels like seconds, reload and resume firing.

"Let's go!" Coney yells, scrambling up to chase several escaping Germans. "They're getting away!"

I join Coney, running through the knee-high brush, firing on the run.

When I have to stop to reload, I see movement to my left. I turn my rifle, finger on the trigger, and almost shoot at Danny Boy. "Out of the way!" I yell at him.

He staggers back, but by now the firefight is over. After fifteen minutes of explosions and rifle blasts, there's silence. Germans lie motionless throughout the brush.

"Don't touch them," Coney warns as we approach, reminding us that their bodies might be booby trapped. The Germans had been known to make bombs out of everything from thermoses to combat helmets. "Watch their hands and kick away weapons."

Unscathed faces are attached to mangled bodies. The expressions of the dead men are consistent; open eyes and mouth, cocked chin, blood caked hair. I don't know if I'll ever shake these images.

"I count fifteen. Let's get back," says Coney.

"Danny Boy!" I call to him, motioning with my rifle for him to follow as we start back.

Danny Boy is standing over a lifeless body. His shoulders slump and his rifle dangles in his right hand. He hasn't yet grown accustomed to killing.

I feel for him. I can still remember the face of a German soldier I killed in North Africa. I try to forget, but I can't. He looked about my age, with blond hair and blue eyes. A lot like one of my baseball teammates back home. I bet he was popular in school, especially with girls. He was staring into the sky, mouth open, head tilted slightly toward his shoulder. A thin trickle of blood flowed from the corner of his mouth. At times I wake up dreaming of being chased by a man with that face.

As we reach the intersection, an ammunition truck explodes. The stench of burning gas and flesh replace the fresh salt of the sea air.

"Yes, sir," Sully is saying over the radio transmitter when we reach him, "we knocked out a machine gun nest and a number of trucks carrying infantry and supplies. Yes sir, we'll continue providing flank support towards Gela."

Sully turns to Doc Ito, who is securing a bandage around Wolcott's right shoulder. "How is he?"

"He's fine for now, but he'll need medical attention."

"Can he walk back to the beachhead?" asks Sully.

"Yes, but he needs to be treated as soon as possible," replies Doc.

"Wolcott," says Sully, pointing over the tree line. "About a mile behind those trees is the beach. Take your rifle and find a medic or mobile hospital. We don't have any way of transporting you. Take care of yourself and keep hydrated." This wound doesn't look like his ticket home.

"Willy," Coney asks one of the other guys in the squad, "what happened at the intersection?"

Willy replies in his heavy Polish accent. "Sully split us up," he says, talking low. "He saw a reflection from a watch worn by a German. He threw in a couple grenades and opened fire on the nest."

The scar over Willy's right eye glistens with the sweat that trickles down from his hair. "Hank and I hit the first truck, then crawled forward to the ridge of the road and popped the second one. Sully killed the machine gun nest with Marty and Romeo. We crossed the road and positioned ourselves for the third truck which turned out to be filled with ammunition. The flames lit up the rest of those trucks like Christmas trees."

"Where's Hank?" asks Coney.

Willy points with his cigarette to a field. "He's staring at dead Nazis, trying to find someone he knows. Just like in North Africa."

"Hank, get the hell over here," yells Sully. "Willy, dammit. Next time, listen for my order. I wasn't in position when you fired on those trucks. Understand?"

"Yes, sir," said Willy with a slight smile, probably because it had turned out all right in the end.

Sully turns back to the rest of us. "We're going to continue on this road, which leads to the town. The skies are clearing. Watch for German planes. Expect more German units from the west. The road to Gela is lined with small farms and fields, with trees along the road. Watch for snipers and machine guns in those farmhouses and trees."

My boots, which had been soaked that morning, are now just damp. My pants and shirt have begun to dry in the hot sun. We move towards our first town. There's still no sign of Lucky.

CHAPTER 4

"Slow down, Arty," Coney yells. "You're walking on my shoes."

Coney's voice startles me, but not as much as the sudden sound of the grinding gears of American Sherman tanks that immediately follows it.

I've been alone in my thoughts for most of our march to the outskirts of the beach town Gela, where we've just arrived.

But we aren't the only ones to discover the tanks. Within seconds of the time we stumble upon them, fighter planes speed out of the high white clouds and dive directly towards us.

"Get the hell off the road!" yells Sully.

"Are they ours?" Coney shouts over the noise.

"Don't ask questions! Dive!" Sully yells back.

I land on the side of the road, bury my head in my hands and curl up into a ball—partly out of fear, and partly to shield myself from the steady thud of machine gun fire up on the road. I hear the massive boom as a nearby tank explodes.

Those poor guys, I think, but I'm too afraid to lift my head.

"Stay down, he's coming back," Sully yells.

I begin digging in the roadside dirt with my hands, trying to escape, as more explosions go off and gunfire pounds steadily on the road.

"Where the fuck are our planes?" Danny Boy begs, shaking.

"Just stay down!" I yell without lifting my head.

Finally, quiet falls.

I slowly lift my eyes, then raise my head. The three tanks on the road are all on fire. No crew anywhere nearby. No one made it out. Those guys never had a chance.

"Let's go," yells Sully. "Get out of here!"

We dart between the tanks that survived the attack, moving ahead with them as they roll forward. At times, I find myself struggling to breathe from a combination of tank exhaust and dust. It looks like Danny boy is, too.

"You okay, Danny Boy?" I ask. He blows his nose and coughs, but nods.

When we reach the town itself, whole sections have been shelled by allied destroyers and mobile artillery. Smoke rises from the surrounding areas, punctuated by the pop of gunfire as we approach the first street.

"Don't pick up any enemy helmets, guns or rifles," Sully warns us. "Always open doors on the left—remember, the Krauts know we Americans enter from the right. And don't use water faucets. Remember your booby trap training. And stay behind the tanks until we get to town."

Groups of Italian soldiers are relaxing in a grove of trees under the supervision of 11th Division infantry. The Italians are dressed in dark brown uniforms with pockets on their chests and helmets that remind me of my mom's salad bowls. The prisoners laugh and smoke. They know they'll be sent to camps soon. Their war is over.

"I call the first Italian sports car," Romeo yells with a smile, walking with his rifle slung over his shoulders and machine gun ammunition hanging around his neck. He looks like a western desperado from the cowboy movies I watched at home.

"I call shotgun!" Marty replies.

"Deal!" Romeo nods with a grin.

Up ahead, there's a huge boom as a tank is hit. I dive for cover.

"Arty, look for snipers," Sully commands as the unit scuffles off the road. "Marty and Romeo, set up on the right. Willy and Hank, focus on the outward buildings."

We begin rifle fire, joining the cacophony from Marty's machine gun. From the second floor, a German machine gun returns fire.

But that's not the only threat. As soon as I see it on the roadside ahead, I recognize the weapon: a single shot launching tube that used to fire directly on our tanks in North Africa.

"Coney!" I yell, "Panzerfausts ahead! On the side of the road!"

Coney tosses a grenade, which explodes on an enemy soldier just before he fires himself. The sound of rifle and machine gun fire continues for a few minutes longer, until enemy guns are silent. Then an American Sherman tank blasts the machine gun placement out of the building.

"Let's go!" Sully yells as he steps back onto the road, moving again towards town.

Despite the shelling, most buildings are still standing. Several have white sheets hanging from their windows to signify no enemy is present. But there's no guarantee we can believe the signal, and some of the buildings are two stories high. I don't like the feeling that we're easy targets for snipers.

We separate on either side of the street, moving forward. I keep step between Coney and Danny Boy. Marty and Romeo set up on cellar stairs on the right side of the street, aiming their machine gun towards an intersection.

"Split up," Sully instructs. "Coney and Arty, Danny Boy and Kelly, go to the buildings on the left. Willy and Hank, come with me to the right. Doc, stay here under cover and we'll call for you. Be careful of civilians hiding, especially in cellars."

As we cautiously walk forward, I hear gunfire at the other end of town. The stench of burning fuel and gunpowder hangs in the air. The sun begins to tuck itself behind the two-story buildings that line the street. The buildings are light in color, with decorative orange, yellow and purple designs. The words El Duce are scrawled in large letters on walls throughout town. As I scan the windows, looking for snipers, I can't help but think what a busy town this must have been, so close to the beach. Without war, I'm sure the patios would be full of people laughing, talking and enjoying themselves.

Up ahead, the last remaining tank turns right at an intersection. We can also see divisional infantry split side by side, beginning the painstaking process of inspecting each building.

Coney and I approach a white stone two story building with a large front window. Over the door, a wooden sign that reads *Forno* rocks back and forth slowly in the gentle breeze. There's only one door, with a rectangular window pane. We squat and peer through the window, but a white curtain hinders our view.

Trying to stay below the window, Coney turns the knob as I crawl to the opposite side of the doorway. The door's unlocked, so the handle moves easily under Coney's hand. I duck and cover, preparing for an explosion or gunfire.

Nothing happens. Still crouching, Coney slowly pushes the door open with the barrel of his rifle. The squeaking of the hinge sends a clear warning to anyone inside.

Empty glass cases line one wall. I smell fresh bread. I guess "*Forno*" means bakery.

All I can think of now is fresh bread, while Coney and I work in tandem, searching for access to a cellar or second floor. I'm the one who finds the door that leads to the stairs to the second floor, so I motion for Coney to join me and we begin our step-by-step climb, each of us walking sideways as we ascend the stairs with our backs against the wall. I'm two steps ahead, my rifle pointing upward. Every creak of every floor board makes me cringe. Beads of sweat begin to roll down my face in the closed heat and humidity of the stairwell. I try to shake them away in annoyance, but with both hands on my rifle, there's not much I can do.

"Damn, you're a heavy breather," whispers Coney.

At the head of the stairs, there's a door. I hold my breath and turn the knob, then give a gentle push.

The door opens on another squeaky hinge that lets out a sound like a car backfiring. Coney runs up the last several stairs, through the open door, to the left. When I follow him up, the hallway is dark and lit only by light from the stairwell. As Coney watches, on high alert, I kick open the first door on the left, and Coney rushes in, ready to attack what turns out to be a bathtub and sink.

Coney steps back out into the hall. Now he takes the lead. It seems like neither of us can take a single step without making the wooden floorboards squeak, but finally he reaches the door to the room at the end of the hall. In a crouch, he's already lifted his right hand to grab the knob when he notices the door is cracked and motions for me to back up.

Then the door flies open and something drops to the floor.

"Grenade!" yells Coney. The door had been booby trapped. We half-run, half-slide down the stairs as the German potato masher explodes. A burst of dust and debris fly into the stairwell, like it's chasing us.

"You ok?" asks Coney, stopped halfway down the steps, between heavy breaths.

I lift my head. "Yeah. You?"

"I may have dropped a load in my pants, but I'm fine."

I wipe my forehead as we resume our ascent into the smoke.

"Let's go to the right and then get out of here," says Coney.

Upstairs again, we don't find anything after checking the right side of the hall.

"The cellar entrance must be outdoors," I say.

Nodding, Coney heads back to the first floor, with me close behind. When we get outside, the sun has set. Headlights from the trucks, small fires and cigarettes provide the only light. In the back of the bakery we locate two metal doors covering a stairwell.

Coney opens the doors and I start to descend the narrow concrete steps. "Where the hell are you going?" he asks me.

"Just follow and shine a light," I whisper.

He follows, rifle in his right hand and flashlight in left. At the bottom, there's a wooden door, the first one in the place that doesn't open with a loud creak. I'm hit by a cool, musty smell. Coney shines his flashlight onto bags of flour, mixing equipment and scattered barrels.

"Looks like bakery supplies," Coney says softly. "*Americano nessun danno*," he adds, then translates. "I'm an American and mean no harm to you."

To our left, something falls.

Coney swings his light in that direction, raising his voice. "*Vieni fuori, Vieni fuori o ti sparo! Vieni fuori o ti sparo!*" I aim where Coney's light is shining. Behind a row of boxes, I see his light reflected in more than one pair of eyes.

"*Vieni fuori nessun donno,*" Coney says.

The two dark shapes stand, arms raised. An older man and woman. I motion for them to come out.

"*Sei Solo?*" Coney barks.

"Si," the couple responds in chorus as they step out from behind the boxes.

As we lead them up the stairs, the woman notices the jagged hole torn in the wall by the fighting, and begins to cry softly. At the top of the steps, a military policeman meets us, eyeing the couple suspiciously.

"They're harmless," Coney says. "They live here." The husband puts his arm around his wife as they walk slowly together around the bakery, towards their front door.

"Where'd you learn Italian?" I ask Coney as we walk deeper into town.

Coney lights a cigarette. "Didn't you read the booklet on Sicily?" he asks. Once again, I'm impressed with his sharp memory. It serves our squad well, and I'm grateful that Sully made Coney my teammate.

As nightfall nears, other civilians trickle onto the streets. Some appear dazed and traumatized, while others hug neighbors in joy and relief. Gela is now in American hands.

Our squad reunites near the northern edge of town, near a field with a grove of trees divided by a stone wall. "Camp near the wall," Sully instructs. "Partner up and alternate watch every couple of hours. Dawn will be here soon enough."

"You need your beauty sleep," Coney tells me. "I'll stay on guard." I unroll my sleeping mat and stretch out, thinking about home.

CHAPTER 5

It was just a year ago, junior year of high school, when I played my last baseball game during the Class B sectional championship of the Capital District of New York State. Winning that game is all any of us on the team had thought about since the season started. It was everything we'd worked for, and everything we dreamed about. When the day came, hundreds of our classmates, teachers and family members cheered from the stands.

My friend Billy was pitching and he threw a fastball to my right. When I shifted my body to catch it, my right cleat stuck in a hole, making my ankle fold over. My glove, which was zeroed in on the ball, rose a couple of inches. The ball hit the lower thumb of my glove and bounced away. I jumped up, flipped off my mask, and slid on my right leg to catch the ball and throw it to Billy, who covered home plate. Billy caught it, but the Scottie from Ballston Spa slid and got his right foot over it just in time.

"Safe!" the umpire yelled, waving both arms back and forth. The Ballston Spa bench erupted and raced to home plate, jumping on the runner who had just scored. I stared at Billy, then dropped my head as I walked off the field. I felt ashamed and responsible. I had failed my team. How could I return to school after losing this game? How could I face the friends and neighbors and teachers who had all just seen me fail?

I left the house early the next morning, before anyone else woke up, wheeled my bike out of the garage and pedaled towards the bus depot, taking my time through the tree lined streets, where mist hovered above the grass. At the bus station, I bought a ticket to Ballston Spa and stashed my bike behind the station.

Ballston Spa's Main Street was bustling when I arrived just after eight a.m. I walked towards the recruitment office, passing a newsstand along the way. A headline from the "Saratogian" caught my eye: "Germans Advance Against British in North Africa." I reached for the paper.

"Hey kid, this isn't a library," a gruff old man growled at me, from under his beat-up old Brooklyn Dodgers baseball cap, a remnant of a cigar sticking out of his toothless trap. "Either buy it or leave it!"

I moved on until I found what I was looking for: the recruitment office. By now, some of the sting of losing the big game had faded. But the feeling I had looking at that newspaper hadn't. Ever since America had joined the war, something had been building in me: a feeling that I couldn't just let other people fight for my freedom. I needed to fight for it myself, and to fight on behalf of others. The disappointment of the big game was what had spurred me out of the house that morning. But something else, something much deeper, was what really brought me to the recruitment office. And it had been growing inside me for much longer than just the day before.

I'd been prepared to enlist—since December 7, 1941, to be exact. Dad and I had just returned home with a six foot evergreen whose fragrance filled the home, competing with the sweet smell of my mom's sugar cookies. I stuck a pine needle between my lower front teeth; it was sharp and pleasantly spicy. Dad set the stand in the far corner of our living room and I held the tree upright while he tightened the screws against the trunk.

My parents' favorite Sunday afternoon show, "Sammy Kaye's Sunday Serenade," played on the dining room radio while Suzanne, Catherine, Dad and I began trimming the tree. Mom was busy baking in the kitchen. I stepped outside onto the back porch to gather a few extra logs for the wood stove. A stronger wind had replaced the brisk morning air and dark blue clouds covered the sun. It felt like snow. I shivered with cold and excitement. Maybe tomorrow would be a snow day!

Back inside, Dad checked on the wood stove and returned to the tree. "Arthur can you grab..." He stopped mid-sentence and focused on the radio.

"*We interrupt this program to give you a special news bulletin,*" a journalist announced. Mom joined us in the living room as he continued. "*The Japanese have attacked Pearl Harbor in Hawaii by air... The attack was also made on all naval and military activities in the principal Hawaiian island of Oahu... A Japanese attack on Pearl Harbor would naturally mean war. Such an attack would naturally bring a counter attack and hostilities of this kind would mean that the President would ask Congress for a Declaration of War... We return you now to your regularly scheduled program and will give you more information as it comes along from the White House."*

Dad turned off the radio, pulled out his pipe and slammed the back door on his way out. The words "declaration of war" lingered in the air. I felt as if I stood in cement. It was as if time had suspended itself and we were all statues. Mom sat down on the couch and began to pray quietly.

The next day in school we listened to President Roosevelt declare war on Japan. A feeling of anger came over me as he described the attack; so many lives were lost. I could feel my body become stiff as I clenched my hands and jaw. By the end of the week Germany also declared war on the United States.

In the days to come, all everyone talked about was the attack. Dinner conversations centered around who enlisted. My friends and I talked less about sports and more about strategies for enlisting early. For a while, our daily basketball games were replaced with watching activity around the military recruitment offices on South Broadway. We were just shy of sixteen. This was going to present a problem. Then my friend, Billy, learned about a guy forging free fake ID's for anyone who wanted to enlist before the age of 18. The following Saturday afternoon a bunch of us went to the pool hall and picked up our fake IDs. None of us, though, had the courage to actually join up. Six months later, I would be the first.

A flag hangs by the door of the recruitment office, waving slowly in the morning breeze, just like the flag that hung off our porch at home. My father worshipped the flag. He knew all the rules around flag maintenance, but I never paid much attention when he rattled them off. More than once I'd wondered why he went to so much trouble for a piece of cloth. But I didn't feel that way now.

My father was a veteran of The Great War. After Hitler's army invaded Eastern Europe, he had told anyone who would listen that he was ready to join the fight, if they'd just take him. "If I was young today," he often said, "I would enlist." He talked about the army as a good career, one I should consider after high school. Since money was always a challenge for my family, college wasn't an option. And after yesterday's game, a baseball scholarship seemed unlikely.

Almost 16, I knew I'd be among the youngest to enlist. But something deep inside told me it was now my turn to serve.

On the door of the office was a poster of Uncle Sam, beckoning me in with his bony right finger. Inside, the office was crowded with guys older, bigger and stronger than me.

"Come in, son," said a man in a uniform. He smiled, but he had a handshake grip that brought me to my knees. "How can I help you?"

"I'm here to enlist," I replied nervously.

"Have a seat."

As I took a seat on a metal chair, I noticed his badge said Captain Douglas.

"So why are you here?" Captain Douglas asked.

"Uh, sir, um, I want to enlist in the infantry."

I thought he might ask me why, but he just smiled. "I was also in the infantry," he said. "In today's army there are lots of opportunities for a young man. Here's a form. Fill it out and come back when you're done."

A few minutes later, I returned the form. He examined my fake ID, flipped the card and looked at me. I coughed, my heart skipping a beat.

"Looks in order," he said with a nod. He pointed to a hallway. "Time for a physical. The changing area is ahead. Strip down to your undies. Come back when you're done."

I was pleased to see no one else was there when I got to the changing room. As I changed, I stared back at posters of soldiers with rifles and bayonets pointed in the air that proclaimed, "Victory in Europe is because of you, the volunteer."

The doctor knocked, but he didn't wait for my answer before he pushed the door open. He was an older man with a stethoscope hanging from his left pocket. A strong cigarette smell wafted from his wrinkly skin and his bifocals glistened against the overhead lamp.

After a muttered "hello," he immediately took my blood pressure, his right hand trembling. Then he turned and coughed loudly towards the wall before returning to examine my ears and nose. If I was a barber, I observed, I could make a living just on his nose and ear hair. I gagged as he pushed a wooden stick onto my tongue. Then he examined my feet. "Ah, no flat feet here. You've got a good arch." He finished with an eye test, which I passed.

As I walked out, Captain Douglas waved. "Arthur, over here."

My mind began to race. Did he find out I was not of age? Was he going to bring me to the Sheriff's office to be picked up by my parents?

"Here's your ID. Welcome to the Army. Watch for a telegram for your bus trip to Fort Benning. I look forward to seeing you at the station in Saratoga."

Then he squeezed my hand again with his powerful grip.

CHAPTER 6

"Arty, is that you?" whispers Hank.

Before I can answer, I hear the unfriendly sound of rifles clicking. I'd thought I was safe, hidden out of sight in the grove I'd found while we were out on patrol of the land around Gela. But now I feel a whole lot less than safe.

"Yes! It's Arty!" I respond, as quickly as I can.

"What the hell you doing?" Sully scolds, bursting into the grove, the other guys right behind him. "We could've shot you. With the low fog we couldn't see whether you were friendly or not."

"Dear Mr. and Mrs. Murtaugh," Coney pipes up, his voice tinged with annoyance. "Your dumbass son was killed by friendly fire. But you'd be pleased to know he died with a helmet full of olives." He slaps the back of my head.

"Shut up," I say, rolling my eyes.

"Share those damn olives," Sully says sharply. "You were almost shot for them."

I drop my helmet to the ground, and the guys hungrily grab every last olive. Though they grimace at the initial bitter taste of the uncured olives, soon the starving soldiers are gobbling them like candy.

I'm not sure why I walked into the grove. Maybe to catch a break from the action. Maybe for a hint of juvenile adventure. Maybe for a taste of home, where I often used to walk through the woods. In the fall I picked pine cones in the forest for my mom's Christmas wreaths. That was probably it. I guess for a few minutes I wanted to feel like I was home.

"Damn, these are the biggest olives I've ever seen," Willy mumbles, his mouth full. "Nice job, Arty."

They're a tastier treat than what our squad has become accustomed to in the past few days. For meals we carry two pounds of daily rations, including pork or beef, dehydrated vegetables, coffee flakes, soup powder, soybean biscuits, fruit bars, sugar, cigarettes, sweet chocolate, chewing gum and a wooden spoon. But the surprising treat of the olives seems to provoke a regular picnic.

"Trade, Danny Boy?" asks Coney. "How about a fresh soybean biscuit?"

"What d'you want?" Danny Boy says.

"Cigarettes," Coney answers. "Or chocolate."

Danny Boy rips the wrapper of a chocolate bar open and smells it, teasing Coney. "Hmmm, so damn good," he says, shaking his head and licking his lips. "Mr. Hershey outdid himself on this one."

Coney throws the soybean biscuit with his customary aim. It smacks the center of Danny Boy's helmet.

Danny Boy smiles, then reaches for the biscuit lying next to him. "That's one hard-ass biscuit," he observes.

Hank laughs. "Dear Mr. and Mrs. Foley, your son was killed by biscuit artillery."

Danny Boy grabs a couple of cigarettes and throws the rest of the pack to Coney.

"Sully, I'll buy the first round in Messina," says Romeo, stretched out in the grass with a car magazine in one hand and a cigarette in the other.

"I'll hold you to it," Sully says, smiling. "And that's an order."

"Marty," Romeo says, "if we can't find sports cars, I'll borrow a German cycle and sidecar. We'll ride through town looking for girls: ah, *belle donne*. We'll be their liberators!" he yells, his voice rising in excitement.

Sully sips from his canteen and wipes his mouth. "I call the second ride," he says. Then he stands and starts roaming the grove. "Arty, show me where you picked those olives."

I head over to join Sully near the tree line, but as I do, I realize it's the first time since we've landed that I've gotten a minute alone with the Sargent. And the question I've wanted to ask ever since the landing rushes into my mind.

I've been holding onto hope that Lucky might join us, that I might see his big grin as he walks out of some grove telling us that he's just fine. But at this point, I know something's wrong. So does everybody in the squad. Nobody's really talked about where he'd gone. That's how you knew everybody believed he was gone for good. But now I just want to know the truth. That is, if anybody knows it. And if anybody does, it'll be the Sargent.

"Sargent," I say. "What happened to Lucky? Does anyone know?"

Sully puts his hand on my shoulder. "Arty," he says, his voice low, "Lucky's dead. He fell into the sea. Some sailors tried to save him. I watched them throw a buoy out for him to grab several times. They shined a searchlight on the water as best as they could. He never responded."

I feel sick in the pit of my stomach. I've seen squad brothers wounded or killed before. But this was the first time I had been given responsibility over someone in combat. Sully ordered me to help Lucky, but I failed. I try to take a deep breath, but a sob gets in the way. "It's my fault, Sully," I say, my voice breaking. "I let him down. I should've told you he wasn't focused at the top of that ladder, damn it!"

"Arty," Sully says, almost as if he's giving me an order. "I saw you with Lucky. You talked to him and then Doc checked on him. You can't change the wind or the waves. You did everything I would've done."

My eyes fill with tears. "Why didn't you tell me on the landing craft?"

"Look at you now," Sully responds gently. "Lucky wasn't the only person you had to take care of that day. You had to take care of yourself. I couldn't have you land distracted. I'm here to do my best to get each of you get home alive. One lesson I've learned by leading soldiers in battle: You'll never get used to someone dying when you're in charge. When someone is killed or wounded on my watch, I feel something inside of me is lost."

"Everything ok?" Coney asks, approaching with a look of concern.

"All's good," Sully says. He picks up his pack and leaves.

"You ok?" Coney asks me.

"Yep," I reply, glancing away so that Coney doesn't see my watery eyes. I just want to be left alone.

"Party's over, fellas," Sully calls. "Grab your gear."

In the distance I hear gunfire and artillery. A convoy of trucks is approaching Gela. Behind the trucks are tanks and additional infantry. Our plan is to continue north and accompany the convoy and infantry two miles to the next town.

I try to distract my mind from Lucky by counting trucks. *One, two, three, four…* There are at least 30. A few drop off infantry before turning back towards Gela.

Sully flags down an ammunition truck and talks quickly with the driver. "Okay, boys," he says, turning back to us and gesturing for us to help ourselves to the ammo. "Load up!"

We secure ammunition into our packs and belts while Sully pulls out his binoculars and faces north. The mid-morning sun has melted away the fog, exposing the hills of inland Sicily. The light brown soil accentuates the dark green of the trees on the hillside.

"Holy shit," Sully mutters. "Kelly, get over here!"

Pulling out his map, Sully begins reading coordinates and grabs the radio transmitter from Kelly. "This is Sargent Spinelli," he says, reporting to some officer in the command center who was orchestrating our piece of the invasion. "Large number of enemy tanks and infantry approaching on coordinates W34 by N24. We'll remain close to coordinates W24 by N14. Roger out."

As he talks, the squad gathers around him, taking in the news. "Everyone stay here," he orders when he hands the transmitter back to Kelly. "We're going to be busy."

Sully races to the back of the convoy, jumps onto the lead tank, and bangs on the hatch. The commander pops out as Sully points towards the hills. The commander looks through his binoculars, grabs his radio and begins communication.

Before Sully has time to return to the squad, artillery whines over us and lands about a mile ahead. Several more volleys quickly follow. Sherman tanks move up, veering off the road into the fields and groves of trees at the feet of the Sicilian hills.

As the convoy trucks leave the road, German aircraft seem to fly out of the sun, firing through our lines. We're pinned down. Our gunfire can't reach them. But theirs can reach us. As bullets hit the ground near my feet, Sully points to the sky, yelling: "German artillery! Get the hell away from the road!"

The sound of the incoming shells is deafening. All I want to do is hide. Explosion follows explosion. The wind from American artillery is accompanied by the thud of overhead gunfire from enemy planes.

German artillery from the hills lands directly in the road we've just fled. A convoy truck explodes behind us. As I run forward, pieces of the truck bounce off my helmet like fiery raindrops.

Sully yells at a truck driver fleeing on foot. "Where the hell are you going? Get back here and fight!"

"I'm a driver, not infantry," the soldier yells back.

"Not today." Sully yanks a rifle and ammunition belt from a dead soldier, and hands them to him. "You're an infantryman now. Move up!"

Artillery shells land ahead of us and behind as we weave through the obstacle course of explosions. The air is full of sprays of gravel, rocks, hot metal and shards of destroyed trees.

Finally, a welcome sight: allied planes flying overhead. Our flyboys return the favor, strafing and bombing enemy artillery, tanks and infantry.

Our advance brings us in sight of enemy lines. We bunch up together at the top of the first rise, uncertain what comes next.

"Wait for the infantry," Sully orders. "Marty, Romeo—set your gun here," he says, pointing to a patch of brush to the right. "Everyone else position under the incline." Sully looks back down the road. "Remember, don't get in front of our tanks or they'll run over you."

I clear some dry grass and branches and prop my M-1 on a bare incline while adjusting the scope. Sweat trickles down my face, and my heart jumps out of my chest when I get my first good look at the enemy through my sight. But they're still too far away. I don't have a good shot.

Someone drops onto the grass beside me. I expect to see Coney or Danny Boy, but it's Willy. "Where's your bazooka?" I ask him.

He responds in his thick Polish accent. "It's here, but the Shermans will fight," he said. I guess we don't need bazookas when we've got tanks. "Today, I'm a rifleman," he says, taking a look at the enemy through his own scope. "Like you."

Then he turns to look me in the eye. "Arty," he says. "You're a good soldier. I want to ask a favor when we're out of here."

I don't have time to ask Willy to explain. Overhead, American and German planes begin to spar in firefights. The cloudless blue sky provides a perfect backdrop for the trails of white smoke. Watching the clouds above, I think about laying on my back in the grass next to my sisters, looking up at the clouds of home and naming their shapes.

Now German tanks roll into sight. Each burst from their cannons is followed by the explosion of one of our tanks or convoy truck. Positioned above, on higher ground, German machine gunners open fire on everything below, including us.

I lift my head just enough to see over the incline and begin firing. After reloading several times, I see Danny Boy to my left. He's face down, trying frantically to hollow out a hole with his fingers to hide. As machine gun bullets shred the ground above me, I crawl over to him. "I need you!" I yell. "Get your head up! Fire back!"

"I can't! I can't!" he yells. The only thing that seems to be able to get him to stop clawing at the earth is the blast of an explosion. Then he covers his ears with his hands.

"I need you to be a part of the fight," I yell. I grab his rifle and fire it in the direction of the enemy.

"Look at everyone," I tell him. "We're all fighting. Get up!" I reload and hand him his rifle. "Now!"

He looks at me with wide eyes. Dirt covers his face. His fingernails are bleeding. He slowly pulls himself up. I stare into his blue eyes, searching for any sign of fighting spirit.

"Come on!" I say. "Let's shoot together!" I aim and fire shot after shot. Out of the corner of my eye, I see him sit up, watching.

Then, after what seems like lifetime, he starts firing too. "Great job!" I yell. "Keep it up!"

I crawl back towards Willy. He stops firing. "Nice job," he says. "That's why I want to talk later."

The noise of battle is everywhere, and relentless. Artillery and tank shells land yards in front and behind the ridge. When chunks of gravel drop around us, Willy and I bury our heads in our hands. But out of the corner of my eye, I can see Danny Boy, still continuing to return fire.

As I resume shooting, a huge blast goes off to our rear. I turn just in time to see the gun turret from a Sherman tank fly off and land a few yards away from us. Flames and smoke engulf the tank.

I fire several shots, duck below the ridge and reload. Bullets continue to pierce the surface of the ridge. The enemy is moving forward and tanks are squeezing us. The boom of artillery is only getting more frequent. If we stay here, we'll all be dead. I hear no commands from Sully, just the constant deafening sounds of war.

CHAPTER 7

It's Kelly who brings us the first word we hear from Sully in what seems like hours. Scrambling across the ridge, passing out ammunition, he's also passing along orders.

"Our squad and other division infantry will maintain the ridge," he tells us. "We can't be pushed back."

Then, before he moves on to take ammo to the next man down the ridge, he stops to speak with Willy in a low voice.

"Hank!" Willy yells as Kelly scuttles off.

Down the ridge, Hank twists to look back at Willy. "Sully wants us to set up the bazookas," Willy yells to him. "We've got enemy tanks within shooting distance."

The welcoming sight of American planes flying lower and inflicting damage to the enemy gives me a burst of confidence. Maybe, just maybe, we'll get out of here alive!

"Take that, you bastards!" I hear Romeo yell at the enemy as he makes a mad dash to move forward, looking for an area to set up.

"Push 'em back," yells Sully as he jumps up over the ridge.

I turn back to Danny Boy, and wave to him to follow. "C'mon!" He gets to his feet and we race together towards the hills.

The reflection of sun off the ground creates visual challenges. We stop and shoot our rifles more for show than accuracy. To shield ourselves from fire, we run behind our tanks. But that means the artillery shells aimed at the tanks explode all around us, seeming to increase with each step. From the sky, our planes continue to inflict damage on enemy artillery and infantry.

I find a shell hole, jump in, and start shooting the retreating infantry. Other members of the squad fire simultaneously, unloading our rifles in unison. As I reload, I spot a German tank commander. I take aim and both my shots hit him, shoulder and neck. He grabs at his neck, then slides, twisting and turning, back down into the tank.

The sound of explosions muffle screams from wounded and dying soldiers. I keep my head down, trying to stay out of harm's way, and kill the enemy. But my concentration is broken by Doc Ito. Out of the corner of my eye, I catch him running towards the last area where I saw Marty and Romeo. Trying not to wonder if someone's hurt, I keep firing away.

When the enemy retreats beyond range of our rifles, we give chase. In the chaos of dusty air, burning tanks and dead infantry, I don't have time to think, only react.

As we reach the enemy's former position, still firing and reloading with practically every step, I come upon a wounded enemy soldier. Preparing to take him prisoner, I approach cautiously. When he catches sight of me, he begins to yell in German. Then he yanks a pistol from under his leg. Before he can squeeze the trigger, I shoot him through his open mouth, then walk on, leaving him dead in a pool of his own blood.

Almost immediately, I spot a German tank crew, running away from their burning tank.

"Halt!" I yell! "Stop! Stop, halt!" *They think they're going to fucking run away to fight another day.* I need to stop them. I position my rifle on my elbows. With my first volley, two fall. Another few rounds take down the rest.

I have no idea how long we chase the retreating enemy. But eventually the shelling stops and the only thing I hear are remote sounds of tanks firing up ahead.

I find a crater and crawl into it, prop myself up, take a drink from my canteen and splash my face. The cool water feels good.

After a few minutes, I notice other American infantry walking back towards where we'd come from. They're looking around, retracing their steps. By the sun, I'm guessing it's close to late afternoon. I get up and walk ahead to check out what's going on myself. The sounds of combat have faded even further ahead and once I see the tanks turning back, I realize this engagement is over.

Something draws me to locate the dead German tank crew on my way back. One of them is lying on his side, staring ahead with his mouth cocked open, blood and dirt covering his face. The other three lie where they fell face first, in pools of blood.

Then I stumble on the wounded soldier who I had to shoot. Suddenly, I find myself kneeling next to him, yelling. "Why did you try to kill me!? All you had to do was surrender and you'd be alive now. Fucking cocky dumbass!"

I stand up again, walk on in a daze. Is this really happening? All I can see is burning bodies and smoke from tanks and trucks.

Coney's near the ridge line when I reach it. His rifle dangles from his left hand and his eyes are fixed in an empty stare. "I haven't found anyone," he say. "Have you found anyone?"

"No," I say. "No one yet."

Then I remember seeing Doc Ito running towards Marty and Romeo's position "Let's go," I say, heading in that direction.

A few minutes later, we catch sight of Doc and Sully in the midst of the smoke and glaring sunlight. They're squatting over someone. When we reach them, we can see it's Marty. He's struggling to speak.

"Where's Romeo?" I ask.

Sully wipes his eye with his sleeve and points. "Over there," he says, nodding his head towards a mangled corpse.

I go to my friend. Romeo's body is in pieces. I slowly bend down and look at him.

"I have his belongings," says Sully. "Start digging a grave."

I pull my shovel out of my backpack. The baked ground is compact. I grunt with each shovelful of gravel and rocks, trying not to stare at Romeo. Just this morning he was sitting with all of us discussing his plans for Messina. Now his dreams are shattered like the pieces of his body. I rest, sitting back on my knees, but my eyes begin to tear so I decide to walk away. With shovel in hand I go over to some nearby brush and pretend that I'm taking a piss. From where I stand, I'm in direct view of the Germans I killed. There's no one near them. All around is destruction. Nothing left to do but pick up the pieces of human bodies and equipment. I wonder to myself if the pieces that I have lost in my heart will ever return.

After a few minutes, I walk towards the shallow grave I'd started. I notice Doc Ito bent over Marty, who's making a gurgling sound.

"Another one?" He asks Sully.

"Yes," says Sully, dropping his head. Doc pumps another syrette of morphine to Marty's leg.

Sully's going through Romeo's things, organizing them into a corner of his pack. As he does, he comes across a letter. When he sees who it's addressed to, his expression turns even more serious. He looks to the sky, then goes over to kneel next to Marty.

"Marty, I have a letter from Romeo."

Marty is coughing up blood, but he manages to grunt and turn towards Sully.

Sully takes a deep breath, then begin to read. "Marty," he says. "If you're reading this you know we won't be riding into Messina together. You're a great friend and made my time in this lousy war fun. There's something I never told you. Like you, I'm an orphan. I grew up in an orphanage run by nuns. Boy could they be strict, and they were happy to see me leave two years ago on my sixteenth birthday."

Marty's eyes open wider as he listens.

"I spent most of my teenage years causing trouble," Sully reads on, "while you spent most of your teen years taking care of your little sister. I wish I knew you longer. You would've straightened my ass out. I'd like to think that if I had a younger brother or sister, maybe I could have been as strong as you. I have given my life insurance proceeds to your sister. I hope it will be enough for you to go back home and not worry about her financially. Focus on your dream of a wife and six kids. Forget this horrible war. But please don't forget me, Marty."

Sully pauses for a moment before reading the last line. "Your Best Friend, Romeo."

Marty's hair is matted with sweat, dirt and blood. Blood covers his right side. His right arm and leg are mangled. But he tries to smile.

Then Sully puts the letter in Marty's hand, and tears begin to roll down Marty's face. What remains of his body shakes with tears as he mutters to himself. Sully bends over to kiss Marty's forehead.

The lump in my throat tightens. *Forget this horrible war.*

A few moments later, Marty's gone, just like his friend. We jam the destroyed machine gun barrel and rifle in the disturbed earth covering their graves and hang their helmets from the twisted metal to mark the site. In time, their remains will be returned home for a proper burial. Sully collects Marty's personal belongings, including Romeo's letter, which has fallen from Marty's hand onto the ground.

How strange that these two orphans will have closure with a proper burial, while Lucky's parents, who lost two sons, will never see them laid to rest.

I can't help but wonder what dreams the German tank commander I killed might have shared with his crew. What city was he from in Germany? Would he have known Hank? Did he like sports, too? Did he have younger sisters waiting for him at home? All I could see was him reaching for his neck, sinking back into the tank. But when his family received word that he was dead, what images would they hold close to remember him?

After hours of constant sensory overload from the sounds, sights and smells of battle, I'm too dazed to weep. Since we assembled onto the landing craft for Sicily, I haven't been able to stop thinking about death for a single moment. Lucky. That's how it started. And now Marty and Romeo. In basic training we were told that *war is to kill or be killed.* In North Africa, I didn't think about death. I thought about how to stay alive. I'm more experienced now than I was then. So why hasn't my combat experience helped me handle death?

I look at Sully. He's older than me, and in charge. I figure he knows how to look at death as a matter of fact, but I see him wiping his eyes, too. The truth is becoming clear to me. On the battlefield, nobody wins.

CHAPTER 8

"Mr. Smith!" I yelled, running from one side of the barn to the other. "Mr. Smith!"

"What's wrong?" he asked.

"One of the cows is having a calf!" I responded breathlessly.

Mr. Smith followed me as I dashed back to the other side of the barn. "Look!" I said, pointing to a cow in her stall, lowing and huffing in distress. A minute before, I had been positive that I knew exactly what was going on. But suddenly I wasn't so sure. After all, I only started working for Mr. Smith last week, right after I graduated from elementary school. "She's going to have a calf, isn't she?" I ask.

Mr. Smith puffed on his pipe and smiled. Then he placed his arm around my shoulder and led me away. "Yes, she's having a calf," he said. "Let's check back in a bit. Give her some privacy."

I continued to clean the barn and shovel fresh sawdust for the beds, listening to the mama cow mooing in pain. My friend Billy and the guys talked about where babies come from, but we didn't know for sure. I peeked through the slats of the mother cow's stall just in time to see a calf tumble to the hay in a gush of blood.

"Mr. Smith!" I call, running halfway down the barn. "The calf is here!"

"Let's go check on it," Mr. Smith called back, following behind me.

I dropped my shovel and ran back to the other end of the barn. As I turned the corner, I found a calf standing on four spindly legs. The mother licked her new charge. The calf just stood and stared straight ahead, moving her jaw like she was chewing.

"Keep your distance and don't bother them," Mr. Smith warned.

Off to my right, I heard a symphony of mooing. I smiled as I saw four calves with open mouths press their heads out curiously through the slats in their stalls. Their raised heads moved in unison with their black and white bodies. The new arrival just blinked back at the barn's welcoming committee. Chills up and down my back—the good kind of chills—as I watched the newest calf take in the new world. A feeling of peace came over me.

"Look at that little girl." said Mr. Smith. "I hope you will always remember today. The beauty of new life. Old as I get, I never tire of seeing a newborn calf." He walked over and patted the mother on her shoulder. "You did a fine job, mama. She'll grow to be just like you," said Mr. Smith.

Then he bent over to touch the calf and motioned me over. "Come here."

As I approached, the calf looked up with her big brown eyes from her black and white spotted face. I touched her cool pink nose and she immediately opened her mouth and began to suck on my fingers. Her warm tongue and small teeth tickled me. I laughed. "What's she doing?"

Mr. Smith smiled. "She thinks you're giving her milk. She'll learn to drink from her mom soon enough." He gently positioned the calf close to her mother's udder. "Here you go, girl." Slowly the calf found a finger-like udder and began to drink. Her mama gazed down, as her tail swatted away flies.

Mr. Smith turned and went back to his work. But I stayed there, fascinated by the farming life and profession. For the first time in my young life, I knew what I wanted to do when I grew up.

"What the hell!" I shake my head and bolt up quickly.

Leaves are tickling my nose. Coney's laughing, holding a tree branch. "Wake up, soldier," he says. "You've been out since we arrived last night."

"That was only a couple of hours ago!" I yell back. Why are dreams I enjoy so short? After so much death and destruction, even some from my own hands, I miss the peace and comfort of the farm.

After we'd helped the graves crew give proper burial to our dead, Sully decided to camp the night on the outskirts of Mazzarino. But it was dark by the time we made camp.

As daylight breaks, I see an American flag hanging outside a stone castle. It's the first American flag I've seen in Sicily.

"Coney, Arty," Sully orders, "check out the castle. That's a perfect spot for a sniper or machine gun. Remember, don't engage the enemy. Kelly, come here. I'll check in with the Lieutenant."

This is not a typical reconnaissance mission. All around us, American tanks and infantry are pouring into the town. So worst case, if there are enemy in the castle, they'll be outnumbered. But in combat you assume the worst and hope for the best.

The sun is rising, and the lifting fog reveals a grove of fruit trees near our campsite. Oranges. I pick two from a low hanging branch and hand one to Coney. Before peeling the fruit, I hold it in my hand like a baseball and wind up for a throw. *What a perfect morning for baseball.*

"Thanks, pal," Coney replies through a mouthful of orange slices. "I need this. My ass is dragging."

"Look at the trees," I tell him. "All in straight lines and full of fruit. I feel for this poor farmer. He can't harvest because of the fighting."

"Arty," Coney says, "Is there something in that orange? We're walking towards a castle that may be crawling with the enemy. I get it. The countryside is freaking beautiful. But keep your eye on the ball."

He winks, and I realize he saw my wind-up earlier. But his little pep-talk does help me get my head in the game.

At the end of the grove, we hide behind several trees to view the perimeter. The castle has two four-story rock columns that remind me of a farm silo with windows. Each column is marred by the fist-sized pock mark of artillery strikes. Thick brush and vines climb from the ground about ten feet up each column.

"We're fifty yards from the first column," Coney says, talking low. "I'll run to the first set of bushes. Then I'll signal you."

The fog has lifted now so that we can clearly see the top of the first column. I lay flat and take aim with my rifle, ready to cover Coney. He races to the next stand of brush, checks the area, then turns and waves. I move forward, closing on the column. Then we both break cover, running to the castle column where we pin ourselves against the sand-colored blocks. Coney gets there first, with me just a few feet behind him.

Quietly, we approach the entrance. Coney motions for me to get down while he moves ahead, but I crawl forward on my stomach, rifle under my chest. I'm not letting him go in alone.

An American soldier comes into the doorway, cigar in his hand. As we approach, he steps out and waves. The insignia and bars on his chest signal his status as captain. "You guys on a recon mission to check out the castle?" he asks with a smile.

"Yes, sir," replies Coney. "We arrived under nightfall, just a couple of hours ago. Saw the flag when the sun rose."

"Understand," the captain says. "I'm Captain Peters of the 11th. We're establishing a communication command post. Come in." He disappears inside.

Coney and I follow him into the doorway, still slightly wary. We'd been expecting to find the enemy, not an American post. We cock our rifles and walk inside where we're greeted by several men with maps and equipment spread out on tables.

Captain Peters picks up a map and points. "We're here," he says, "in Mazzarino. The town is large enough to support a command post and mobile hospital. The 11th will continue north to cut off German and Italian armies heading east. Who's your Sargent?"

"Sargent Spinelli, sir," Coney replies.

Peters smiles and rolls the cigar to the corner of his mouth. "Tell Sully that Com Pete says hello. You guys are under one hell of an infantry Sargent. He's one of the best. Learn from him and you'll stay alive."

"Yes sir," we say in unison, and salute.

"As the Krauts retreat," Peters tells us, "they'll eventually make a stand in one of these towns further into the hills." He taps the map, indicating where danger might lie. "Be careful." He returns our salute, and we head out the way we came.

When we get back to camp and Coney gives him the update, Sully grins at the greeting from Captain Peters. "Story checks out," he says. "The town is in American hands. Let's take a look at this medieval castle and say hello to Com Pete."

"Sully, when are we heading out?" I ask, trying to determine if I've got enough time to take a look around town before we go.

"Be back in an hour," Sully says. "Got it?"

"Yes," I say. "I'll be back."

CHAPTER 9

A steady flow of trucks and jeeps enter town as I walk in alone on the main road, which winds through rows of two and three story stone buildings. The morning sun illuminates the buildings' bright colors against a backdrop of green rolling hills.

Further into town, the buildings get even bigger and more vibrant, jeweled with extravagant balconies, decorative pottery and hanging baskets that burst with brilliant flowers that remind me of our front porch during the summer.

I cross the busy street between two convoy trucks. On the other side, I see a large cathedral down a side street. As I walk towards the spectacle I notice a paved circle in front: a perfect spot for a game of street baseball. The cathedral and large buildings on either side are the only structures on the street. The church is several stories high, with a rainbow of marble running up and down its face, under a majestic bell tower and cross.

At the sound of footsteps, I glance over my shoulder. A beautiful girl is heading towards me.

My hands start to sweat and I can feel my heart beat faster. She's dressed in a white head scarf, top and skirt. I look around for a place to hide, but we're the only ones on the street, so I start practicing phrases to myself. What again is *hello* in Italian? Ah, I remember. I begin feeling more confident as she approaches.

I remove my helmet. "Belle donne."

She stops and smiles. "Grazie."

I suddenly realize I just told her she's beautiful. *This is Romeo's fault,* I think. *He was always repeating the phrase.* My heart twinges at the memory of Romeo, and I'm grateful for the pretty distraction in front of me. "I'm sorry," I tell her. "I mean, good morning."

"Ah, buongiorno," she replies.

"Yes. I don't mean you're not beautiful." I begin to confuse myself. Her white dress complements tan skin, silky brown hair and brown eyes.

"You're beautiful," I say, then try not to wince. The more I talk, the deeper I dig my hole. "I'm sorry. I can't talk straight. My name's Arthur."

Softly she replies, "My name is Angelina. I speak English."

Now what do I say? I wipe my face with my sleeve. "Sorry, I'm a little warm." I try to shake myself out of this trance and ask, "Where you heading?"

She replies, "I'm going to the church. Do you want to come?"

"Yes! That'll be great. But I can't stay long. I have to get back."

I fall into step beside her, heading for the beautiful façade ahead of us. "Do you work at the church?" I ask. *Ugh—idiot!* I chide myself.

She smiles. "Yes," she says. "I'm a postulant."

From the confused look, I'm sure she can tell I have no idea what she's saying. "Wait," I say. "Are you a nun?"

"Yes," she says. "I'm studying to become accepted as a nun."

I'm starting to put the pieces together. "You'll be a nun when you graduate," I say.

"Something like that," she says.

She opens the large wooden door to the church. Inside, it's spectacular. Stained glass windows capture the sunlight and throw a colorful rainbow onto the altar and the front pews. Large statues placed throughout the church are adorned with lighted candles. But the air is stale and musty, full of the scent of melting wax.

"Wow," I say, looking at Angelina. "This is beautiful. The largest church I've ever seen."

"It is beautiful," she says. "I'm very lucky to be here."

"What are the other buildings?" I ask. "The ones outside?"

"One is a house for priests and nuns," she tells me. "The other is an orphanage. That's where I live."

"An orphanage?" I repeat.

"We have thirty children. All orphaned by Germans. I take care of them—feeding, bathing, schooling. But I like play time the best."

"That sounds like a lot of fun," I tell her. "I'd love to teach those kids some American sports, like baseball and football." I wish I could stay but I know I need to move. "I'd like to learn more but I have to go," I tell her. "It's been a pleasure meeting you."

She nods. "Likewise."

I hold out my hand. "I'd like to come back." Then I worry she might think I'm being too forward. "I mean, to see the orphanage," I add.

She takes my hand with a smile. "I would enjoy that," she says. "May God bless you. And be safe," she adds.

What a dumbass I am, I think as I walk away from her, out of the church. *I want to see the orphanage. Damn—it's easier for me to fight Nazis than talk to girls.*

Walking through town, I can't get her out of my mind. She's dedicating her life to serving others. She's smart, thoughtful and pretty. She speaks both English and Italian perfectly. The orphans aren't the only thing I'd come back for, if I can find my way back to this town one day.

But the thought of so many kids growing up as orphans because of this war brings me down.

I can't imagine what it must be like to grow up without parents. Despite my challenges with my dad, I'm glad he's around. He and I didn't always get along, but we did agree on one big decision.

The day I enlisted in the army, I arrived home at 3pm. My sister, Suzanne, was reading on the porch. She's the most bookish of the family. Can't get enough of her Nancy Drew mystery stories. "Is mom or dad home?" I asked.

She shook her head but didn't look up from her book.

"Where are they?" I asked.

She paused and sighed, letting me know she was annoyed with the interruption. "Mom is at the market," she said. "Dad is working on Dr. Walter's porch."

Second generation American Irish Catholics, my dad worked by day as a laborer in a manufacturing plant, while my mom worked part-time jobs and was a homemaker with a large garden. But in his spare time, Dad also did odd jobs for a neighborhood store and family doctor.

I opened the screen door and walked in the house, suddenly realizing I was starving. In the fridge, I picked out a Coca Cola and also found a lumpy package wrapped in butcher paper: chicken legs for tonight's barbecue, I guessed. Those were a favorite of my father's and mine.

I grabbed an apple, sat on the recliner in the living room, and placed my drink on the table.

As I sat there, leaning against a comfortable pillow in such familiar surroundings, anxiety welled up in me. *What have I done?* I thought. *I'm underage. I just enlisted to fight soldiers who are older, bigger and stronger than me.* The worry was overwhelming. But more than anything, I needed to tell my parents.

Maybe they would deny my enlistment and contact the Captain, I thought. *Yes, of course—that's what they'll do! I won't need to go, but I'll reap the benefits of having enlisted. Dad will be prouder of me than ever, knowing I didn't just sit back and let others fight. My mother will be so grateful that I'm not going that she'll extend my curfew. My sisters will agree to do all my chores. I'll be seen as a patriot in town and a hero in school.*

Suddenly, my day started looking brighter. I had practically planned a whole new life for myself when I was jolted out of my daydream by the slam of the screen door. When I jumped up, I saw my youngest sister, Catherine, going upstairs. A nearby clock told me I had fallen asleep for an hour. This time, when I walked into the kitchen, my mom was at the kitchen sink. She must have seen me asleep on the recliner and chosen not to wake me.

I suddenly felt an overwhelming urge to take in the backyard view. "Hi, mom." I raced past her, out the back door. There were the lilac bushes lining the back of the yard, the vegetable garden to the right of the back porch, soon to be bursting with tomatoes, peppers, carrots, green beans and corn, with flowers between the rows for color, everything from sunflowers to petunias. Those flowers were Catherine's pride and joy, but I wouldn't be around to enjoy the sunflower seeds she roasted this year, or to tie the dried corn stalks to the porch railings for Halloween and Thanksgiving.

"Arthur," my father said. He didn't know it, but he was interrupting my attempt to lock in memories. "What're you doing?"

"Nothing," I told him. "Just enjoying the..."

He broke in before I could finish. "Bring out the charcoal and lighter fluid."

I grabbed a bag of charcoal and the can of lighter fluid from the tin can where we kept it on the back porch, then walked over to where he stood by the grill and started stacking a small volcano of charcoal up on the grill. "Dad," I asked, excitedly, "Can I light the grill?"

"Not till you're sixteen," he said, with a shake of his head.

I poured lighter fluid over the charcoal. He lit a match and a comforting smell rose from the grill as silhouettes of orange and yellow flame began to dance in the gentle breeze. Within a short time the charcoal whitened and the fire was ready. Part of me wanted to say something right then. *But why ruin dinner?* I thought. Instead, I walked into the kitchen and picked up the plate of chicken legs mom had stacked. She was frying potatoes on the stove; the slices popped and sizzled in the oil. Homemade bread baked in the oven. All of my favorites.

Damn, I think now, walking down the side of this dusty Italian road. *I'd cut off one of my fingers to smell that bread and potatoes again.* I can picture my mom standing at the oven dressed in her flowered apron, stirring the potatoes. I would love to hug her again like I used to when I was little.

"Grab a can of Schlitz on your way out," my father had called on that far-off night.

That was the first of a few he had that evening. My father was a quiet man except when he drank. By his third can he would be smiling one minute and arguing the next. He'd been working harder than ever in the past year, spending more time than he ever did before at work. Drinking seems to take the edge off.

A cool brisk breeze wafted through the yard as mom set the picnic table. She spread out a cotton flowered table cloth and methodically laid down five plates on top. Silverware clicked and clanked. The sun sank behind our neighbor's pine trees. I closed one eye and then the other to see the sun glimmer through the leaves and limbs.

The chicken legs Dad placed on the table were blackened just the way I like. I piled my plate high with thick slabs of bread and a giant helping of fried potatoes, and then went back for seconds. After dinner, my father sat puffing on his dark cherry wood pipe, which gave off the familiar sweet smell of tobacco smoke. By now we'd put on sweatshirts, as the night turned cool. I knew the end of the evening was near. It was almost time to get ready for bed. On any typical Saturday, a feeling of security would come over me as I brushed my teeth and put on my pajamas. But this was not a typical Saturday.

"Arthur," my father said. "I may be able to get you a summer job at the plant that pays more than working for Mr. Smith. I think that would make the most sense."

Dad never liked to hear my stories of animals and farming. He wasn't interested in my two favorite activities: playing baseball and working on the farm. When I tried to tell him how much I enjoyed working for Mr. Smith, Dad either ignored me or rolled his eyes. "You'll have no off days," he always told me. "And farming is not worth the pay." I didn't argue with him, but I felt sure I didn't want to work in a factory.

"Dad," I said. "I read the Germans keep advancing in North Africa against the British."

"Ah, those damn Nazis will never stop until the Americans arrive and take care of business." Dad shook his head. "Just like in the Great War. The tide of the war changed when we arrived. I'm proud of those boys who went off and served." He looked at me. "I heard that Jack Jones's son enlisted last week. Dr. Walter's son, too. This will be another tough war, but with young men like them fighting, we'll prevail."

I drew a deep breath and hoped my Dad would be just as proud of his own son for enlisting. "Dad," I said. "There's another young man entering the war. I enlisted today."

CHAPTER 10

"Arty," Coney yells, when I get in sight of the camp again. "Where the hell have you been? Check your ammo and supplies. We're leaving."

I quickly refill my ammunition, but all I can think about is Angelina. I've never had a real girlfriend, and I failed miserably at my only real attempt. Back home I had a crush on a girl named Rose Marino who sat next to me in algebra. Rose was the smartest girl in class, and she was also beautiful. One day, when she leaned over to help me with an equation, I blurted: "wanna go out? I mean… can I…" She seemed confused as I stuttered, and after a moment of awkward silence we both looked away and never mentioned the incident again.

I'm relieved that my inability to carry on a conversation without blabbering something foolish didn't deter Angelina from saying she would see me again.

Sully is talking with a tall, thin man who's holding a mine detector. To the east the intensity of the artillery increases, and so does the sound of air support.

I manage to get my gear packed up just before Sully calls us all over for a brief. "Gather up!" he yells. When we crowd together to hear him, he goes on. "In the castle, I had a detailed discussion with divisional communications and the Lieutenant," he tells us. "The enemy are retreating northeast. They're setting mines on roads and destroying bridges to slow our advance. We're going to be supporting engineers on the road leading to Barrafranca."

He turns to the tall man with the metal detector. "I want to introduce you to three divisional engineers," Sully says. "Because of our experience, we'll again provide weapons support and assist in dismantling mines." That's exactly what we'd been doing in North Africa. It wasn't safe, but at least it was familiar. I felt a strange sense of comfort in that. "Sargent Olsen will review the plan."

"Thank you, Sargent," Olsen says to Sully before turning towards the rest of us. "Please call me Mel, everyone." He gives us a brief smile, but his face turns serious as he dives into the plan. "Reconnaissance planes have seen factions of the enemy laying mines and charges on roads, on bridges and on railways. A large number of squads of engineers, infantry and armor will combine efforts and remove devices within a four mile distance between towns. We'll continue north and work in conjunction with those to our east. Joining me are Corporals Taylor and Banks. Sargent Spinelli and I talked. We've divided ourselves up accordingly."

Mel reminds me of Sully. He's confident but not arrogant. He speaks to us as men not just soldiers.

The squad divides into groups: Willy, Taylor and Hank; Sully, Banks, and Kelly; I'm with Coney and Mel; Danny Boy will provide additional support and cover Doc Ito. The sun's at its high point, baking us yet again as we advance on the road.

As Coney and Mel talk, my thoughts remain with Angelina. What's she doing right now? What game is she playing with the kids?

"Arty, what're you doing?" Coney yells.

He's standing a few steps behind me, near Mel. "Nothing," I say. "Why?"

"Sargent Olsen said stop."

"Oh, sorry," I sheepishly reply.

Coney doesn't think it's funny. "Get your head back in the war," he whispers sternly, "or you'll get us killed."

"I'm fine," I whisper back, angrily.

Then Mel motions for the two of us to both get down on the side of the road, to cover him while he checks a section of road for mines.

Mel moves ahead, taking slow, ginger steps: first his right foot, then his left. He grips the top of the minesweeping device, which reminds me of a shovel, and waves the plate side to side. The pack hanging by his side swings back and forth, clanging against his belt. Lying in the grass, Coney and I scan the surrounding landscape for enemy movement. From beyond the trees that surround us drift the sounds of tanks idling as other infantry squads and engineers spread out on roads and through the fields. I calculate that we will be doing this until the mechanical mine-sweepers are able to catch up from the beach.

"Stop moving," Mel says calmly. "I have one. Arty, crawl over slowly. Use your bayonet to check the ground in front of you, on one side and then the other, as you approach."

I turn to Coney. "Did he say me?"

"Yes," Coney says. He's the lucky one, but he still sounds stern. "Get moving. Don't leave him alone."

I unlatch my bayonet and crawl towards Mel. When I reach him, I hand him my bayonet and turn to crawl back.

"Where do you think you're going?" he says. "I need your help with this Teller. I only have two hands." He grins. "Get the joke, Arty?"

"Yes, Sargent," I say. "But you're not funny. These mines can blow off tank tracks."

"Don't think of that," Mel instructs. "Just focus." He points at the metal disc half-hidden in the ground. "Dig around the mine with your bayonet," he says. "They're like a dinner plate." I take a deep breath, but my hands still shake as I dig.

"Be gentle," Mel says. "Steady. Use a back and forth motion."

The sun is beating on us. There's no shade to be seen anywhere on the main road. Sweat drips from under my helmet into my eyes but my bayonet's jammed under the mine now, and I can't let go of it to rub them. "Damn," I say. "My eyes are burning."

"You're doing fine," Mel says. "Just another few inches. Ok, release the bayonet, slowly. Now wipe your eyes." I've barely managed to take a swipe at my burning eyes when he goes on. "Remove the bayonet and set it down. Gently put your hands underneath the mine. Don't touch the top. I still have to dismantle the fuse."

"If you're trying to get me to relax," I tell him, "you aren't."

"You're doing well," he replies. "Just stay steady."

Just as I get my hands around the mine I hear the *whoosh* of an incoming shell. It lands with a bone-shaking blast close to the road.

"Get down!" Sully yells from the other side of the road, where his group is also moving slowly forward. "Mortars!"

"Steady, Arty," Mel says. His long, thin fingers move fast, cutting the wires to dismantle the mine. Like a combat surgeon under fire, he gently removes the last component and clips the final wire. In the distance, some enemy tank catches sight of our position and starts to fire. Bullets rattle and shells explode all around us.

"These mortar guys aren't very good," says Mel. "We're an easy target, but they can't zero in."

"Enemy half-tracks!" Sully yells.

The fire from the German half-tracks along with the mortars pin us down. Then machine gun fire joins the explosions, which seem to be everywhere.

"We need to get off of this road!" I yell.

Mel responds so calmly you'd think he was fixing a car in the comfort of his own garage. "Just a minute," he said. "We're done with this one. But the Germans plant mines in groups. There'll be more. Move ahead. Grab your bayonet and slowly check the ground to the left and the right as you crawl forward."

It's the last thing I want to do, but I know it has to be done. If we don't clear these mines, they could take countless lives.

I turn and keep my head low, moving up. The air is full of the smoke from Sherman tanks, which also turn up dust as they speed around us, chasing the half-tracks. Mortar shells continue to rain down.

"If these were the Herman Goering division mortar crew, we'd be dead," Mel says. He's stayed back, still searching for mines. "This mortar crew must be inexperienced Germans who got left behind."

Lying on the road, he moves the mine sweeper back and forth. "Another one, Arty."

I crawl over.

A couple hundred yards away, Sherman tanks stop and fire along a small ridge. An enemy half-track is hit and explodes. That same Sherman returns to the road further ahead. Within seconds—*kaboom, kaboom*—the Sherman explodes.

"Damn it!" yells Mel, as he finishes dismantling another mine. "If these mines weren't here, we could have gotten there to save those guys! Keep working, Arty!"

This was the first time I've seen emotion from Mel. But his anger isn't at fate, or anyone else. It's with himself, for not being able to remove the mine in time. Like Sully, he takes each death personally, and takes the blame. You never hear them shift responsibility to anyone else. Soldiers like Mel and Sully continue to teach me every day about being a better soldier and man.

Gunfire and shells continue to rain down on the road. I bury my face, still holding a mine for Mel to dismantle as bullets skitter across the road and buzz over us.

"This one's done," Mel says. "Keep moving."

"Shouldn't we head off the road?" I try.

Mel doesn't even respond. He just continues to wave the mine sweeper, his head and upper torso exposed to the fire on the road. I follow him, with my head and rifle at ground level, digging with my bayonet.

"Sargent," I yell. "We need to get off this damn road before we're both dead!"

"Arty," Mel says, not taking a break from his methodical work. "Stay the course. If we miss one of these mines a truck full of infantry will die. This is war. There are no shortcuts."

I know he's right. Teller Mines and Bouncing Bettys are randomly placed and will destroy any vehicle or soldier. We'd just seen proof of it, when the tank ahead of us hit a mine and blew up.

Crawling after him down the road, I find myself falling into a zone of focus, despite the sounds and the shrapnel. I know that if I made one small slip, I'd die too. Somehow that has a way of focusing your attention.

By my count, we've now pulled out twelve mines, all now heading for the junkyard.

"Arty, another," Mel says, turning to me. We've done it so many times now that it's starting to feel familiar.

But in a split second, Mel drops to the ground and the gravel around him turns red. I crawl over with my bayonet yelling "Doc! Doc!"

Mel gasps, coughing up blood, holding his throat and rolling back and forth. He's got a bullet through his neck.

"Doc," I yell. "Where are you!" As I turn to the left to scan for Doc, he dives onto the scene from my left.

"Let go," Doc yells, pulling Mel's hands away from his neck. "Let me see."

Machine gun fire continues all around. Danny Boy fires back in their direction.

Doc does a quick inspection of Mel's wound. "The bullet missed his spine," he says to me. "Hang in there, Sargent," he encourages Mel. As he sprinkles powder on the area and stuffs gauze and bandages in the wound, he nods back at me. "I'll give him one morphine," he tells me. "Arty, there's a church in Mazzarino set up as a temporary hospital. Find a way to get him back to it. There must be a jeep behind us."

"Ok, Doc!" I stumble as I try to regain my balance, then run towards the back of the column.

Wait a minute. A mobile hospital at the church? Despite the seriousness of Mel's wound, I can't help feeling a charge of excitement. *Angelina may be there!*

"Hey, hey!" I yell, waving as I run towards a soldier in a jeep. "There's a wounded engineer who needs to go ASAP to the mobile hospital."

Before he can do anything I jump in the jeep. "I'll ride and assist," I tell him. "Go!"

He drives up, avoiding the dismantled mines. With Doc's assistance we get Mel into the jeep. The fighting has moved a couple hundred yards up the road. I'm so focused on saving Mel I barely hear the explosions and gunfire still going off in the distance.

"Arty," Doc yells. "One more. Kelly has mortar shell fragments in his right leg. His foot's bad."

"Where?" I ask.

Doc points to Kelly, leaning against a nearby tree.

"I need to stay here for the other wounded," Doc tells me. "When you get there, have the jeep return." His face looks grim as he thinks ahead to the rest of the battle. "We'll have more wounded by then. Stay at the hospital. Be a pain in the ass to the physicians and nurses so Mel and Kelly get good treatment. Got it?"

"Yes, Doc!" I yell, racing towards Kelly.

"I'll tell Sully," Doc yells back. "Be safe."

When I get to Kelly's tree, Danny Boy is already there, bent over, trying to pick Kelly up. "You need to go on the Jeep," Danny boy tells him.

"I'm so tired," Kelly says.

"Kelly," Danny Boy yells "Get up!"

Kelly tries, but he has no energy. If we move him, he may lose his dangling foot. Doc has tied a tourniquet above the wound to slow the bleeding.

"We have to carry him." I tell Danny. "Even if it costs him the foot. Otherwise, he'll die. Better to lose a foot than a life!" Danny nods and slides his arms under Kelly's upper body; I scoop up Kelly's good leg and use it as a splint for the damaged one. We get him in the Jeep, and I hop in and crouch down between Kelly and Mel.

"Arty," Kelly says. "Tell them to save my foot. How can I work when I get home? And what girl is gonna date a cripple?" Tears run down his face, either from his fear or his pain, or both.

"Be strong," I tell him. "You're getting out of here. You're going home. Soon you'll have home cooking and be sleeping in your own bed."

Kelly nods and smiles as he tilts his head back against the seat.

"Let's go!" the driver yells.

I glance over at Mel, who's struggling to breathe through his wounded throat. I can see the fear of death in his eyes. "Mel, look at me," I tell him. "Think of how many lives you saved today."

Mel is one of the bravest men I've ever met. Just thirty minutes ago, his steel nerves kept me calm and alive. Now I need to return the favor.

CHAPTER 11

The engine roars as we come around a curve and I bounce against the metal side of the jeep. Kelly and Mel both writhe with pain from the jolt. I struggle to keep them from sliding around like I just did, but there's only one of me, and two of them. "Driver," I yell. "Can you slow down!"

"Do you want these guys to live?" he yells back.

"Mel," I say. "Focus. Kelly, stay awake!"

As the Jeep careens around vehicles and infantry, I feel my fingers yanking in their sockets while I stretch to keep one hand on Kelly and the other on Mel. Both men have bled a tremendous amount. They're having trouble staying awake.

"Stay with me!" I yell.

Mel's fallen off the seat and is lying sideways on the floor. I adjust his body, trying to get him into some position that looks comfortable. The driver speeds up. The road is now a straightaway. After a few miles, I see a white sign with a red cross posted along the roadside. When we reach it, the driver makes a right and we come to a screeching halt, slamming my backside into the metal rod yet again.

The driver carries Kelly inside, a trail of blood marking his path. Still in the Jeep, Mel has lost consciousness. I pick up his limp body and he can only muster a faint breath. As I carry him into the church. A familiar musty smell greets me.

"I need help! I have a man bleeding to death!" I yell.

"Over here," yells a man wearing a bloody white coat, waving me over towards a cot.

I carefully place Mel down on the cot. "Shot to the neck," I tell him. "Our Doc bandaged him and gave him one morphine syrette."

The doctor from the church is already doing his own inspection of Mel's wound. "Doesn't appear the bullet hit the spine," he says. "He's able to move his lower body. But he's lost a lot of blood." He glances my way. "Okay, soldier. I have it from here." Then he's looking around, gesturing for one of the women standing nearby. "Nurse!" he calls. "Bring plasma and sutures."

I move out of the way and try to catch my breath. Cots and IV poles are scattered around the church, but the altar candles are still lit and the rainbow colors still shine through the stained glass. Next to the altar is an area screened off by curtains, with bright lights glinting beyond them. As I watch, a pair of orderlies quickly move Mel into this area.

I notice the Jeep driver has turned up now, too, standing near me. "Where's Kelly?" I ask him. He points as he heads for the door, about to take another run to collect more wounded.

"Thank you, buddy!" I yell.

Kelly's lying on a cot with an IV in his arm. He's unconscious. If I didn't know better I would say he's sleeping peacefully.

"Can I help you?" asks a woman dressed in blood-soaked green scrubs.

"I'm in the same squad as Private Kelly," I tell her. "Ma'am, will he be ok?"

Instead of answering right away, she looks down at Kelly. I notice the shine off of a gold pin with a red N on her collar. Then she looks back up at me. "Yes, soldier," she says. "He'll live. But he's going to lose his leg from the knee down. He's lost a lot of blood but the tourniquet slowed the bleeding. The fluids will hydrate him."

She must have seen how I felt about this on my face, because she held out her arms and gently gave me a hug. "Son," she said, "you've done well. You saved your friend's life."

"Thank you, ma'am," I say, hugging her back. I'm in a daze. I haven't been hugged since my mom wrapped her arms around me at the bus station over a year ago.

Then she stepped back and gave me a once-over. "You should wash the blood off your hands," she says, before moving off to help another soldier.

But before I can worry about washing up, I need to check on Mel.

I find him behind the curtains. As I slowly pull the fabric aside, I see a clinical team working on him.

The doctor looks up without a break in his work. "Are you in the same unit?" he asks.

"Yes sir," I say. "How's he doing?"

"He's lost a lot of blood and the bullet punctured his aorta," the doctor tells me. "He's bleeding at a faster rate than we can replace. I'm sorry, son. We'll ease his pain." He sticks another syrette into Mel's leg, then stops working. The doctor pauses to place his hand on my shoulder for a moment before he heads off to attend to the next soldier.

I go with Mel as he's transferred to a quiet area. Others near him lie under white sheets, covered from head to toe. They're heading home to their final resting places. Mel's not gasping anymore. He seems at peace. His eyes are shut and he looks like he's sleeping.

I reach into his front pocket and remove his belongings: a picture and some letters. The picture is of Mel, smiling as he holds a baby, with a young boy standing next to him. A blond-haired woman stands beside Mel, her arm around both him and the boy. A note at the bottom reads, "Merry Christmas from the Olsens: Mel, Shelly, Mel Jr. and David." I tuck the picture with the letters in my pocket. Then I remove Mel's wedding ring, along with his watch. I'm sure his wife will appreciate having the ring. And his sons will treasure the watch. I place them in my mom's lilac bag.

I hold Mel's hand and bend over to kiss him on his forehead. His breath is slow, but I can still feel it. I didn't know this man this morning. But in that short time, he'd taught me duty, focus and maturity while under intense fire. And he's dying now so that others can live. Damn war.

Mel is the first soldier I've known with a wife and children. I begin to tear up, thinking about what it will be like for his wife to receive a telegram from the war department saying Sargent Mel Olsen was killed in action on July 14, 1943. Mel's young sons will grow up without a father. Most likely, they won't remember much about him.

"Would you like to pray for him?" I'm startled to hear a soft voice, and even more startled that I recognize it. Angelina is standing next to me. I hope she can't see me crying. I quickly wipe my eyes.

"Yes," I reply.

She lifts her left hand. "In the name of the Father, Holy Ghost and Son," she begins. Then she prays several Our Fathers and Hail Mary's. In the midst of them, Sargent Melvin Olsen, Sr., a husband, father and soldier dies on a cot in a church in Mazzarino.

Angelina continues to pray, but now that Mel is gone I feel a strong urge to check on Kelly. And I know I've got to get back to the squad. With these losses, my friends need all the men they can get.

When I find Kelly, he's still unconscious. I look around for a nurse to leave him a message. "Please tell him his buddy Arty was here," I tell the nurse when I find one. "Tell him the whole squad wishes him a quick recovery and safe trip home."

Then I head for the nearest door out of the church, desperate for a quiet moment and a breath of fresh air.

But when I glance back to take one last look at Kelly, I see Angelina's there, praying over him.

CHAPTER 12

I step out the side door of the church. The air's humid, but it feels good, cleansing my lungs of the hospital smells. An orange horizon gives me the clue that night is imminent. I empty my canteen over my head and hands, hoping to remove the dried blood. If only it could wash away the memories of the past few hours, too.

I know I have to rejoin the squad, but all I want to do is sit. *Why wasn't I killed?* I wonder. *I don't have a wife or kids. Why am I alive while Mel is dead?* My mind is full of the sight, sound and smells of death and destruction, and my heart is heavy with sadness over the loss of so many friends.

Sitting on the bottom step, I wrap my arms around my legs and let my head drop. As I do, I slowly begin to take in the sights of the yard. A well-kept stone fence protects a flourishing vegetable garden, several trees full of colorful citrus and a well for water. I wander over to the vegetable bed and squeeze a red tomato, ready for picking. I kneel in the cool dirt and pull a few weeds. The smell of the earth and vines takes me right back home, to the days when I helped my mother in her vegetable plot as a boy. I sit back on the grass of the churchyard and remove my hardened boots, stripping down to my bare feet. The soft thick grass feels good on my soles, set free from a prison of wool and leather. I place a thick blade of grass between my teeth and lie back, staring at the sky, trees and birds.

After a few minutes, I pick a grape from a nearby vine. The sweet taste permeates through my mouth and entices me to select several more. Their sweetness mixes with bitter olives I find on a churchyard tree. For dessert I enjoy the smooth taste of fresh-picked almonds. After my snack I lie back in the thick grass. In the sky, several stars have come out now. I close my eyes. For a few moments I can almost believe I'm home, camping in my back yard with my friend, Billy.

"Are you ok?" asks that soft voice. Angelina sits on the grass beside me and takes my hand.

Her hands are soft and clean while mine are still bloody, dirty, callused. I suddenly realize I must smell terrible. But her presence relaxes me. Suddenly, we're talking, in a way that I've never talked with anyone before. I tell her about home: baseball, my sisters, Mr. Smith's farm, the lilacs in our yard. I smile and feel like the teenager I am. If I could have, I would have taken her to a malt shop or a movie. But I'm grateful for these moments in the churchyard.

"Angelina," I ask her after a few minutes of conversation. "I bless myself with my right hand but you used your left. And your order of Father, Son and Holy Ghost was different than what I'm used to saying. Is that how it's done in Sicily?"

She looks down. "No," she said. "Sometimes I forget the order. Or which hand to use."

I'm surprised that she can forget these details, if she wants to be a nun. "Why do you want to be a nun?" I ask. I expect a quick response, but instead she sits, staring.

Now it's my turn to ask her if she's okay.

When I do, she begins to cry. "I'm sorry," she says.

Did I make this amazing person cry? I wonder. "What's wrong?" I ask. "Did I say something wrong?"

She stands and walks away, sobbing quietly. I feel helpless. It always upset me when my mother or sisters would cry, even if I wasn't the cause. In this instance, though, I sense that my question triggered Angelina's sorrow.

I get up and walk towards her. "Angelina?" I try again.

She turns and looks at me, her cheeks stained with tears. "It's not you," she tells me.

I nod, relieved but suddenly embarrassed and uncertain about what to do next. *Maybe I should go. I need to get back to the front soon, anyway.* I strap on my pack and pick up my rifle. As I begin to turn and leave, Angelina stops me.

"You're observant and smart." She grabs my hand tightly, leading me into the yard toward a large fruit tree. No one's around and she whispers, "I've had to keep quiet about my past and I'm tired of it. I want to be myself again. I want to laugh and have fun again. This war has taken so much of my life. I'm tired of lying. I've been on the run since leaving Rome. At the end of 1940."

I start to pull my hand away, surprised by her deception. But she tightens her grip.

"No," she says. "I'm not a criminal. I'm Jewish. My mother is Jewish. Her family moved to Rome so my grandfather could teach at the University. She met my father there. He was a soldier."

I sit in silence as she explains her past. Angelina tells me that she's sixteen and has a little brother Mario who is eleven. They were a happy family until the Fascist regime of Mussolini took over and aligned with the Nazis in 1939.

I had heard from Hank's experience of the anti-Jewish stance of Nazi's and now Angelina's life story reinforces the importance of stopping this hatred. But I never understood the magnitude of their hate until now. Angelina's Jewish grandfather had colleagues at universities in Warsaw and Prague, she told me. It was his colleagues who told him about the arrest of Jewish families who were then sent to work camps throughout Europe. Angelina's story opens my eyes to the impact on Sicilian and Italian civilians, everyone living in the countries that have been consumed by this war. She's a girl on the run, owing to no fault of her own.

As Angelina continues, she becomes more animated. "My parents sent me to a girl's school south of Rome," she continues. "The fascists watched our family's every move. They wouldn't question my leaving for education, but how could we explain Mario disappearing? They knew he was in grade school and had no reason to leave, so my father took a chance and faked that Mario caught the fever and died. A loyal family friend who was a doctor wrote up the report and death certificate. At the burial, my parents were terrified that the fascists would open the empty coffin. But once it was buried, they left us alone.

"Then my father and brother picked me up near the school. We obtained passage on a train to Naples and stayed with a family friend in Ariano Irpino. My father returned to Rome to be with my mother, but my brother and I studied in the home of our friend, and worked every day on a dairy farm.

"This worked well," she went on, "until the number of Nazis increased in the Avellino province. Finally, in June 1941, Mario and I boarded a ship as steerage and arrived in Messina, where my father's oldest sister was a nun. She helped us. Mario is one of the children posing as orphans, and our parents now live on the same farm."

"Once the Germans leave Sicily," she says, smiling for the first time since she began to tell her story, "my family will be together again."

She takes a cautious glance back at the church door. Then she pulls a star from her garments. "It's the star of David," she says. "A symbol of my faith. My grandfather gave it to me."

She kisses the star and begins to cry. To comfort her, I place my arm around her. She rests her head on my shoulder as she cries. After a few minutes, she sits up and wipes her eyes. "I'm sorry, Arthur, to tell you all of this after what you've been through. My problems are small in comparison to what you see each day. You're so nice to me and when you're around I feel like I'm home talking to a boy in school." She wipes her eyes with the back of her hand. "Also, you're a very good listener. I've been rude," she continues.

I'm about to respond, to tell her that I am glad she shared her story, when a voice calls from the church.

"Angelina! Angelina, where are you?"

"That's Mother Superior," Angelina says, scrambling to her feet. "I'm sorry. Before I go, please take this." She hands me a small metal box. "Use this when you're in war."

I open the box to find a rosary similar to my mother's. At the sight of the smooth beads and cross, I feel immediate comfort.

"Keep this close and you'll have God's protection with you all the time," Angelina says.

My pack is already full, but I do not want to lose this gift. Then I have an idea, "I'll put the rosary around my neck," I tell her. "That way, God will always be close."

She smiles. "That's even better." She bends down to wrap her arms around me and squeezes. Her hug feels different than the nurse's. I pull her closer and she kisses my cheek.

"I'm sorry," she says. "I didn't mean that."

I smile and rub my cheek.

Angelina is already running towards the church. "Thank you again for listening," she calls over her shoulder. "Be safe and God bless."

I take one more look around the churchyard. I hope this will not be my last visit. Standing eye-to-eye with the top of the stone fence, I pull myself up, climb over, and drop down onto the street.

CHAPTER 13

On the little Italian street, I can't help but reach up to touch my cheek where Angelina kissed it. I am a great listener. That's a first. But when I think about the happy portrait I painted of my home life, I feel foolish. We haven't been through anything as challenging as what Angelina's family has faced. I think back to my own toughest night.

"Dad, I'm leaving this week for Fort Benning, Georgia. I'm going into the infantry." We were still sitting in the back yard after our barbeque, but it felt like a heavy load had come off of my shoulders. Dad just sipped his beer.

"You're not of age," he finally responded. "How'd you do this?"

"That's not important," I told him, with a confidence that surprised me. "What matters is that I'm enlisted." I stared back into his eyes, trying to be firm. He opened a new can with a click and took a gulp, but said nothing. I was used to my father not saying anything. He rarely talked other than to tell me what to do. But I felt uncomfortable in this silence. He stared straight ahead, the back porch light illuminating his face. The load that had just slid from my shoulders landed squarely on his.

After what felt like hours, he turned towards me.

There was fear in his eyes. "Son," he said, "why did you do this?"

I hesitated. I didn't want to hurt my father with the truth. He waited, but I remained silent.

"Dammit, Arthur!" he finally exploded. "War's not a game. Why did you do this? Answer me!"

"I enlisted because of you!" I burst out. "All I've heard for the past two years, was you saying if you were young enough you would enlist and kick Nazi ass. You said any young man worth anything would have enlisted! Since before Pearl Harbor, you've said it's our responsibility as Americans to eliminate evil from the world. Even tonight at dinner you were saying how Mr. Jones and Dr. Walters have such fine sons, because they enlisted."

My father just sat there. Then his eyes began to tear and he held his head and bent over. I didn't know what to do. I'd never seen my father cry. My own eyes began to tear up. "Dad, this was no big deal." My tone was more pleading than I intended. "You and your friends would have done the same if you were my age."

My father went still and quiet. "Actually," he began. "I did do the same thing. In 1916. I was hearing all the patriotic bullshit from old men and I decided to leave high school and enlist. I forged my father's signature. My parents weren't happy, but they knew I was determined. I left physically ready, but not mentally. I was too young to comprehend what I was getting myself into. At the movies I watched the reels of soldiers dressed in pressed uniforms being treated like heroes as they went off to war. Families waved at the train station. In fact, I accompanied several of the older kids in the neighborhood on the way to their deployments before me." He took another sip of beer. "We were foolishly excited. War seemed like a big adventure. It interrupted the daily grind of school, of work, of being a kid. I wanted to grow up too fast. I had never been out of this part of the world. Europe was exciting. But what I experienced was very different from my childish fantasy."

My jaw fell open. My father had told me he was born in 1897 and enlisted at the age of 19. *Why had he never told me the truth? Maybe he didn't want to plant ideas in my head?* How ironic that I've followed in his footsteps, while he turned into one of the old men who filled his own head with thoughts of war so many years ago.

As Dad resumed speaking, his tone shifted. "Don't tell your mother I told you," he said sternly. "We had just started dating when I enlisted. She wasn't very happy. She threatened to not take me back if I returned. Of course, she changed her mind." He winked, his tone softening. "She also made me promise that if we ever had a son, I wouldn't encourage him to make the same mistake."

He picked up his pipe and puffed twice. The comforting sweet aroma settled back over the table. Our neighbor's dog, Brownie, barked as he trotted towards our back porch. My sister Catherine opened the screen door with a plate of dinner scraps for him. Crickets chirped under the porch as night fell.

In the long silence, I hoped that when I returned from the war my father and I would share a common bond that many fathers and sons don't have. We would swap war stories. My Dad would proudly introduce me as his son, the soldier. In that moment, I felt as if I made the right decision.

Finally, my father spoke. "I'll tell your mother."

"Arty!" someone yells. "Is that you?"

My thoughts, and the darkness of the Italian street, are broken by the flash of a lighter. Standing directly in front of me are my squad brothers, Jazz and Country Boy, who's holding up the lighter. The last time I'd seen them was in the midst of battle in North Africa, when Doc Ito and I helped them get out from under the fire of a German machine gun. But they'd been separated from the squad since then. We greet each other like long lost friends, shaking hands and exchanging pats on the back.

Corporal Chandler "Jazz" Rodgers grew up in upstate New York. He's the squad musician and keeps us up to speed on the latest hits. I'll never be able to forget his favorite tune, *Lazy River*. Thanks to him, I've heard that song several hundred times a day for months. Private First Class Jimmy "Country Boy" Black is from North Carolina. He's the first southerner I've ever met. His drawl takes getting used to, but his laid back attitude carries into combat. He's one of the calmest guys I've ever met in the face of battle. But one warning: watch your boots. He spits tobacco, and his aim isn't very good.

"You'll be a boost to the squad," I tell them. "We've had three killed and two wounded in the past few days." Their faces change at this news, and I quickly tell them the casualties we've suffered.

"We're being sent back to the squad as replacements," Jazz told me. "We've got to find a jeep ride going that way."

"Great!" I say. "You mind me tagging along?"

Country Boy looks askance at me. "You stink, son," he says. "And your uniform is a mess."

"Thank you for noticing!" I say. He laughs and takes a spit at my boots.

"Jazz, you look even stronger," I tell him. "The hospital must have treated you well. I still have to look up a couple of inches to see you eye to eye."

"Yeah," Jazz says. "It was a nice break. Once the wound healed I definitely had fun in Oran." He winks. "But I couldn't wait to get back. I belong here with the squad. We've got some unfinished business." His smile turns serious as he drags on his cigarette.

We find a jeep heading in our direction. Country Boy's ready to jump into the front seat, but his head's an inch or so taller than the windshield.

"You need a step stool to get in?" Jazz laughs. "Damn, did they reduce your height in the hospital? I don't remember you being so short. Why don't you get in the back with private Arty? Arty, help Country Boy up into the jeep." Jazz climbs in on the passenger side, laughing at his own jokes.

"Asshole," mutters Country Boy. "If I'm so damn short, you're lucky I don't punch you in the nuts."

I'd missed this banter. These two were best friends, yet complete opposites. It's just part of the makeup of our squad: guys from different parts of the country coming together for one cause. If we were back home, we would never have met.

We head back along the same route we took on the crazy drive to the hospital. This time I'm able to relax, staring up at the sky as a crescent moon tries to outmaneuver several clouds and light our way. I'm serenaded by Jazz's whistling and the grinding of gears. I close my eyes as the cool breeze hits my face. The hum of the jeep is soothing, not loud enough to prevent conversation. Country Boy stares ahead and routinely spits while Jazz keeps the driver alert, asking questions.

"You been busy?" Jazz asks.

"Yeah," the driver responds. "Steady. I've been bringing replacements and wounded back and forth. I just dropped off a couple of military police to Barrafranca. They're looking for a soldier who committed a crime back home."

"Who?" Jazz asks. "What'd he do?"

"Nah," the driver says. "I didn't ask."

In the distance I see the shadowy buildings of a town. We're dropped off on the outskirts. "Here you go, fellas," the driver says as he brings the Jeep to a stop. "Welcome back to the war."

Darkness blankets the area. The only lights are from passing vehicles and cigarettes. "Sully," I call out. "Coney, Danny Boy, you here?"

"Over here," whispers Coney.

"Look what I found in town," I announce happily as the three of us head towards his voice.

"Jazz and Country Boy!" Coney yells, as they emerge from the darkness behind me.

He leads us to the squad, sitting in an open area about twenty yards off the road.

Sully excitedly shakes hands with Jazz and Country Boy, patting each hard on their back. Sully and Doc had enlisted with the two of them before the war and they all became good friends. *Maybe*, I think, watching Sully's genuine reaction, *a part of himself has come back with their return.*

"Did you go home?" Coney asks.

"Nah," Jazz says. "We stayed in Oran to recuperate."

"Well, better than landing in a hurricane," Hank says. "At least you missed that fun."

"Y'all would've liked my spitting in the wind that night," Country Boy says, laughing. "To hell with your boots. I would've aimed high, with the wind at my back."

"Country Boy," jokes Sully, "if I'd seen you spit, I would've pushed your ass into the sea."

"I've never been that sick in my life. I had nothing left in my stomach," I add.

Country Boy and Jazz rejoining us is the shot in the arm the squad needed. When your squad brothers leave with severe wounds, you wish the best for them, but you're never sure if you'll see them again or even whether they'll survive.

For fifteen minutes we forget about the war and are old friends sitting around a campfire. It's a welcome respite to the rhythm of war. Coney brings me up to speed: while I accompanied Mel and Kelly to the hospital, the squad had continued working with engineers to clear the remaining road. When they entered Barrafranca, it was deserted by the enemy.

The only one missing from the ring around the fire is Willy.

As the conversation continues, I notice a cigarette being lit in the darkness, out of the corner of my eye. In the flare of the flame I see Willy's face. I walk over. "Don't you want to say hello to Jazz and Country Boy?"

"In time," he replies.

"Everything all right?" I ask him. Then I remember something from the battle. "You asked me for a favor in the foxhole."

"Not sure why I picked that time to say that," Willy says. "I think it was the first time since we got here that I thought I might not make it."

"What kind of favor do you need?" I ask him.

Willy took a couple of drags on his cigarette. The glow highlights his scar. As he exhales, smoke accompanies his words: "Arty, I killed a man."

"Willy," I tell him, "we've all killed men. We might not like it, but that's what we're here to do."

"No, Arty," Willy says. "Not in combat. Back home in Pennsylvania. I killed my father's supervisor."

There is silence between us.

"I see," I finally say, trying to sound calm. But my hand reaches anxiously into my pocket and closes on the only thing it finds there: a stick of gum.

"All I wanted to do was talk," Willy says, talking now as if he can't quite stop himself. "My father was hurt while he worked on a machine. They just fired him and told him to not come back."

The more he speaks, the louder he gets. "Shh," I tell him. "You don't want Sully coming over. Let's move further away." Suddenly, I feel weight on my shoulders, this time through no decision of mine.

We slip between some trees. "I worked in the same factory," Willy continues. "One night, I noticed the supervisor's office light was on and the door cracked open. I went to have a look. He was sitting with his back to me, sifting through papers. I walked in quietly and leaned against the wall. He was drinking whiskey. When he saw me, he laughed. He poured another drink and laughed even harder. Drunk." Willy draws a sharp breath. "I told him he owed my father an apology and a job. That he had brought pain and shame to my family."

Then Willy locks eyes with me. "Arty," he says. "I was going to walk out the door. But then the son of bitch said, 'Ah, you're the dumb pollack's son. What the hell do I care about him or your family?' And he pulled out a pistol and started waving it in my face.

"I still didn't do anything," Willy told me. "But then he started laughing. 'You're stupid,' he yelled at me. 'Like your father is stupid.'"

"I could tell he had too much to drink. I wasn't sure I could get out of there without him shooting me. So I grabbed a paper weight from his desk and hit him on his head. But when he fell back, he hit his head on a steel radiator. When I knelt down to help him up, there was blood everywhere. I froze. I didn't know what to do. And then I felt his chest had stopped moving.

"I tried to get his heart going again, but there was so much blood. I panicked and ran. I went home, left my savings in an envelope for my parents and enlisted the next morning. Then I jumped on a bus as fast as I could." He wipes his brow and takes a deep breath as he lights up another cigarette.

I don't know what to say. Willy, quiet, looks at the ground. Trying to process the story, I begin walking back towards the others. *A murderer? No, that's not the Willy I know. It was self-defense.* I stop and turn back towards Willy.

Suddenly, something I heard earlier that day falls into place in my mind. "On the way back here," I tell him, "the Jeep driver said there are two military policemen looking for a soldier who killed someone back home."

Willy freezes, then speaks slowly: "Thanks for telling me."

"I know someone in Mazzarino who may be able to help," I tell him. "Her name is Angelina. She's a postulant at a church."

Willy's eyes open wider. He nods. "I don't have any other options, that I can think of." He thanks me.

Whatever happened that night, I couldn't accept that Willy was a cold-blooded murderer. "Tell her that you're in the same squad as Arthur. But I'm going to level with you. If you touch her, I'll come looking for you."

Willy stretches out his hand and we shake on the deal.

"Arty, you've treated me better than I deserve. I give you my word, if I meet Angelina I'll be a gentleman. When I disappear, please don't say anything to Sully or anyone?"

"I'll keep this our secret," I promise. "Just take care of yourself."

We drift back to the group in time to catch our new orders from Sully. "Get ready to move out," he says, breaking up the friendly circle. "There's heavy enemy movement to our east. Jazz and Country Boy, man the machine gun. Coney, carry the radio. Be ready in five minutes at 2300 hours."

CHAPTER 14

Later that night, I feel rain for the first time since the landing. The shower quickly becomes a downpour. A warm wind propels the heavy rain sideways, creating havoc for any motorized vehicle. Rivers of water run down towards us from the hilly terrain. Despite dark and the weather, we've been moving at a fast pace for a couple of hours.

"Keep your rifles dry," Sully routinely reminds us. The rain pounding off my helmet and the ground muffles his voice.

On the muddy incline of the road, even the most sure footed soldiers sometimes slip and slide back down. Our boots squish with each rhythmic step.

A loud explosion occurs ahead. Sully turns. "Either one of our vehicles hit a mine or German artillery is firing on the front of the column," he barks. "We're going to be busy. Coney, bring me the radio."

Coney runs up so Sully can update the Lieutenant. Light flashes ahead. If I didn't know it was artillery fire, I might think it was the lightning of a summer thunderstorm.

"Arty, doesn't this look like fireworks on the fourth of July?" Danny Boy observes.

"Yeah," I say. "But these fireworks are trying to kill us."

"Thanks for ruining the moment," he replies.

In just this little exchange, the explosions have already grown closer to our position.

"German artillery is targeting the field!" Sully yells. "Spread out! Watch out for machine gun fire."

I glance over at Danny Boy. "You doing ok?"

From the light of the flames of battle, I can see his face. "I'm fine," he says. "Don't worry. My rifle's loaded. I'm ready."

"Just checking," I reply. Danny Boy has come a long way as a soldier since our landing.

Fifty yards ahead, a Sherman tank explodes.

"Keep your head up," Sully yells. "Watch for enemy infantry following the tanks."

The next explosion is only twenty yards away. Then it's followed by multiple impacts. As we move, we can hear the rattle of a German machine gun, closing in on us. The downpour has diminished to a light shower but the damage is done: the field we've got to fight in is nothing but mud.

I spot a safe zone between tanks. "Over here," I call. With the enemy coming from the west they'll be to our left. Darkness covers the killing zone, except for numerous lights from machine gun tracers, artillery, tank gunfire and a growing number of burning vehicles.

When I duck between the tanks, shells continue to land closer, and at a faster rate. Danny Boy's still to my right. I run from cover, trying to take shots along the way. But a lone soldier shooting in all this chaos is like a fish taking a stand in the ocean.

"Damn it!" I yell as I trip and fall. I don't need an injury right now. I push myself up and quickly work off the ankle pain, coughing from the smoke and stench of battle. Sherman tank fire strafes the open area directly in front of me. I dive for cover, keeping watch for other tanks that might inadvertently run over me.

Now I start to hear the *whoosh* of American artillery shells from behind us as they sail overhead, towards the enemy.

Sully's voice cuts through the chaos. "Jazz and Country Boy," he commands. "Over here. Everyone else spread out and stay low."

In the light from an artillery shell explosion, I find an open area, dive into a trough and prepare to shoot. I prop my rifle on the higher ground and squeeze the trigger: *pop, pop, pop*. Machine gun tracers blaze through the night on my left, right and above on higher ground. Shells fall around me in the grove, and the trees groan as they explode, their branches turning into wooden shrapnel as deadly as any arrow.

On my right I can see tracers from Jazz's machine gun. Someone jumps into the position next to me. I turn, ready to fight, but the light from an explosion reveals the intruder to be Danny Boy.

"Welcome to our ready-made foxhole," I tell him. "I'll shoot to the left and straight and you fire to the right."

The number of shells landing behind us intensifies. To my left a Sherman tank takes a direct hit. Flames lick out from under it before anyone can escape.

"Move ahead!" Sully yells.

In the fiery light, I see Jazz's silhouette running forward, carrying the machine gun, while Country

Boy follows with ammunition. I turn to Danny Boy, and shout, "Let's go! We need to keep up."

As I run, he trails me. With each step, I try to avoid the path of tracer bullets. "Get down!" I yell, as a German tank drops a line of machine gun fire just ten feet ahead.

When the firing stops, I run in a zig zag to the cover of a clump of trees. Danny Boy's still to my right. The light from burning tanks flickers on a cluster of fresh stumps, the remains of several trees.

"No shooting!" I yell to Danny Boy. "We don't want the tank to see us."

I grab my canteen, but my hands are shaking too hard to open the top. I feel like I have night chills. But when I touch the rosary around my neck and think of Angelina, my hands become steady. I open the canteen and splash my face. The cool water feels good. When I look back at the battlefield, the German tank is moving away.

Planes buzz overhead. "Ours or theirs?" Danny Boy asks.

But in the dark, it doesn't matter. No one can tell who's an enemy and who's not. Machine gun fire from above pounds the ground around us. Then one explosions lands too close. "Get out of here!" I yell.

Without a plan, I move forward, just trying to maneuver around stumps and continue to avoid tracers. Immediately ahead, tracers from a German machine gunner begin to fire.

I turn to warn Danny Boy, and my legs are taken from under me.

I fall forward. Somehow, I manage to throw up my left arm to shield my face as I hit the ground. But as soon as I land, someone jumps me, pushing my body to the ground. I get my arms free and turn over to face my assailant, but when I do, his large hands squeeze my neck. I grab his fingers to break his grip, coughing and gasping for air. My body rocks from side to side, trying to get free. I grab for my rifle, but it's nowhere to be found, so I grab up fistfuls of dirt—stones and anything I can find—and throw them at his face. In the glint of an explosion, I see the silhouette of a German helmet and a face twisted with rage, a large scar running from his nose to his lower cheek.

He yells, his eyes wide. His chest is much larger than mine. Damn it. I can't breathe. I can't stop him. As air escapes my body, I begin to feel faint, but I keep on trying to kick and punch. He spits in my face. Will this be the last thing I ever see? Images of my family, Angelina, and the newborn calf in Mr. Smith's barn begin to drift through my mind.

But with a sudden rattle of gunfire, the strength in his hands is gone. He drops on top of me. I feel warm liquid oozing down my neck. I take a deep, unsteady breath, then push the German off me. Blood flows from his head and neck. He's dead.

I'm still trying to catch my breath as I crawl on my stomach, trying to find my rifle, which I finally see by the light of an explosion nearby.

When I find Danny Boy, he's crouched nearby, firing at the enemy. "Did you kill that German?" I ask.

"Yeah," he says. "Sorry it took so long. I had to kill his buddy first."

"I owe you my life," I reply.

I can see how much stress he's been under by his sweaty hair, clumped under his helmet. But he doesn't even stop shooting when he says, "Arty, you've kept me alive since we landed. We can hug it out later. Get to work and shoot!"

The roles have changed. The student is now the teacher.

Ahead, we see machine gun tracers, clearly giving away the position of the guns they're coming from. I pull out two grenades and yell, "Cover me!"

I approach the machine gun nest from the left. Between the dark and the underbrush, I can't see anything. But I can hear each of the bullets as they whiz around me.

Damn, they've changed their direction. I crawl forward until I'm within five yards of the gunner's position, and wait for them to reload. Then I toss a couple of live grenades, and dive for cover.

Both grenades explode, one after the other. Then the nest is quiet. I race up and push the dead away, looking for the gun, but wary because I remember that a working machine gun can feel as hot as open flame. But when I find it, it's clear the damage from the grenades have ended the war for this weapon.

"Over here," I yell.

Danny Boy joins me behind several stumps near the cleared machine gun nest. Within seconds, we're surrounded by explosions and machine gun fire.

"We need to keep moving," I tell him. But before we can, a thunderous explosion goes off to my right, throwing me back onto the ground. My helmet flies off as and my head bangs the packed dirt. The concussion from the blast dazes me. I lay on my back, staring at the sky. Tracers and artillery create fireworks overhead.

After a few minutes I begin to collect myself. But I realize I haven't heard anything from Danny Boy. I find my helmet and begin to crawl forward, cradling my rifle in my arms, calling, "John! John, where are you?"

"Arty." The faint cry comes from just ahead.

I crawl towards it. "John!"

"Arty." The voice is closer now. "I can't see! I'm rubbing my eyes. Can you help?"

When I get to Danny Boy, his right arm and leg are gone. Five minutes ago they were strong limbs. Now they're just a pile of mangled flesh and bones. What have I done? I think, in shock. If I hadn't told him to move ahead, he'd be fine.

"I'll help you," I say. I pour water on his face, then settle the canteen in his left hand, the only one he's got now. "Use this hand," I tell him.

"Thank you," Danny Boy says. "That feels better. But I still can't see! I'm getting cold. I don't want to die. I have so much I want to do. Don't let me die, Arty!" He starts to cry.

"Medic!" I yell. "Medic!"

But in the chaos of explosions, no one hears me. I pull out my kit and stick a syrette into his only leg.

"Please take my letters to my family," Danny Boy says. "They're in my pocket." He nods towards his right. I open his pocket and remove them.

I hold his hand, trying to keep my own head down. Despite the continued explosions and machine gun fire, I can see his lips move as he sings softly, "Oh Danny Boy, the pipes, the pipes are calling. From glen to glen down the mountain side." He interrupts himself to cough and spit blood.

"Arty," he says. "Please sing with me." I open my mouth but can make no sound. "The summer's gone and all the roses falling," he continues. "It's you must go, it's you must go, and I must bide. But come ye back when summer's in the meadow."

Crying, he grips my hand and stares at me. "Arty, please don't forget me," he says. "You're a good friend. Please make sure my family gets my letters. Will you promise?"

"Yes," I say. "I will. You saved my life, and I'll never forget you. You're one hell of a soldier."

He tries to smile and squeezes my hand tighter. Then he coughs and continues to sing, "But if you come, and all the flowers are dying… and I am dead, as dead as I well may be, you'll come and find the place where I'm lying…" He grabs my hand even harder and arches his back in pain. "I'm sorry, mommy," he calls out, "for not coming home!" Then he takes his last breath.

I have no choice but to leave him there. There's too much fire by now to stay, so I move forward, in and out of holes, chasing the retreating enemy. All around, tanks and vehicles are on fire. But with every advance, the machine gun fire and explosions become fewer. And as the fighting finally moves forward with retreating Germans, we turn back to the battlefield.

In the light from burning vehicles, I return to Danny Boy and dig him a shallow grave. I remove his ammunition and stick his rifle in the ground, bayonet first, then gently hang his helmet and dog tags on it. I grip the rosary around my neck and kneel. For the first time in a while I lower my head and pray. When I'm done, I smile as I remember Angelina blessing herself. When I finally rise, I say one last goodbye to Danny Boy. "May we see each other again, John. Peace, my brother."

As I stumble through the dark of the recent battlefield looking for the squad, I'm overwhelmed by the night, so exhausted I can't walk any farther. I decide to take a break in the safety of a hole. As my eyes drift shut, I remember past July 4th celebrations in Congress Park.

We always walked to the park as a family. Mom would pack a picnic basket full of sandwiches, potato chips, Coca-Cola, and beer for dad. Once we got there, I played football, hide and seek, and war with my friends.

But when the show started, I rejoined my family and watched the beautiful lights, shapes and explosions with amazement. Everyone but dad was happy. He was always tense and sometimes the loud explosions made him jump. I used to get angry with him. Why was he miserable on such a beautiful evening?

But I'd overheard him talking my mom when we got home. "I experienced enough fireworks in the foxholes," he told her. "I don't like loud sounds." Then he'd go out into the backyard and sit alone in the dark.

Now, as I lay in this hole in Sicily, I understand how my dad felt.

CHAPTER 15

I'm lying flat on my stomach, my pillow under me, my hands propped up, pretending they're a gun. With cover provided by my bed sheets, my battle had started. "Charlie, watch for the enemy," I told an invisible friend, then pretended to fire my machine gun while I imagined enemy shells landing all around. "Cover me, Charlie," I say, then imagine myself running to another spot. Then I rearranged my pillow onto the bed, and resumed firing.

I was always wound up after an evening of fireworks and games of war with my friends. But my imaginary battles only lasted a few minutes before I fell asleep, hugging my pillow. The next morning I would wake up in the same position, but during the night those dead enemy bodies had always disappeared.

Now I squint against the morning light, waking up. "C'mon mom," I complain. "Shut the curtain. The sun's in my eyes."

"Arty," Coney says. "I'm not your mom. Get up. You doing ok?"

The rising sun reveals a scene out of a horror movie. Heavy, smoky haze covers the area. I see vehicles ablaze, destroyed trees, gaping holes in the landscape, and bodies everywhere.

"It's a mess, Arty," Coney says. "How did we survive? Look at all the dead Germans. They outnumber us two to one."

I scan the area, then point to a shallow grave. "Danny Boy died over there last night."

"Damn," Coney says. "He was a good guy. Willy's gone, too. I heard Hank say he ran ahead during the shelling. This morning there's no sign of him. He must have been blown to bits."

"Anyone else?" I ask.

"Nah," Coney says. "That's all I've heard. We did take some prisoners. Hank's watching them," he says, pointing at a group of men not far from us. Then he looks back at me, with concern. "Are you sure you're not wounded? Your neck and shirt are covered in blood."

"That's a dead German's blood," I tell him.

Then I'm distracted by the fact that Hank's over there talking to the prisoners he's supposed to be guarding, but with his gun down. Apparently Sully notices this about the same time I do.

"Coney, Arty," Sully says. "Glad you're here. Get the fuck over there and replace Hank. Some of these prisoners are SS. They'll trick him and jump him. Don't fall for their bullshit."

As we approach, Hank's smiling, speaking German.

"Hank," Coney yells, pulling him aside, away from the prisoners. "What the hell are you doing? They're the enemy. They killed Willy and Danny Boy. Why are you laughing with the fucking SS?"

Hank looks down. "They're my former countrymen," he says. "Not all of them are bad. In fact, one of them is from Munich. He only lived a few blocks from me."

"Sully says we're taking over," Coney tells him sternly. "He wants to speak to you."

"I can protect myself," Hank responds angrily. "I'll watch them. Tell Sully thank you for his concern, but I'm fine!" Hank turns and walks back toward the prisoners.

Coney chases him down. "Don't be an asshole," he yells. "Sully gave an order."

I stand with my rifle aimed at the prisoners as Hank storms away.

"How's it going, Arty?" Doc asks as he comes by. Jazz and Country Boy arrive just behind him.

"Guarding prisoners," I tell him. "I buried Danny Boy this morning and I have his personal items for Sully. Did you find Willy's body?"

"No," Doc replies. "I asked around but no one's seen any trace of him. There were so many explosions last night. And as you know he didn't shy away from danger. We probably lost him to a shell."

The prisoners I'm watching are smoking feverishly, their hair messed up and their faces dirty. I can't help but agree with Hank. I'm sure all of them are not evil. What option did these guys have, other than being a soldier? Either you fight or your family will be sent to a work camp and never seen again.

"That's a baker's dozen," says Coney as he returns.

"Huh?" I ask

"Can't you count?" he jokes.

"Ok, I get it," I say. "Thirteen prisoners. Damn, you're too smart for the infantry. With your wit and intelligence you should be in artillery."

"I just stay here because I know I need to watch over you so you make it home, Squirt," Coney kids back, with a punch in my shoulder. "Hank will be a good lawyer. He's making a strong case to Sully for him to watch the prisoners."

"What's he saying?" I ask.

"He's saying he'll be able to talk to them so they can understand how well we care for our prisoners. Also, we'll be in accordance with the Geneva Convention if he can oversee them until the military police arrive."

"What's Sully saying?" I ask.

"He's listening and nodding."

A few minutes later, Sully arrives with Hank. "The MP's are ten minutes away," Sully informs us, then starts to give orders. "Coney and Country Boy, grab ammunition off the truck beyond those trees. Jazz and Arty, stay here and keep your rifles on them. Hank, talk to them quietly, but stay at least ten feet away, do you understand?"

Hank nods reluctantly.

Ten minutes later, there's still no sign of the MP's. Hank's talking and laughing with several prisoners. Trucks and infantry start to arrive in the mid-morning sun. The idling of Sherman tanks further out in the field is a welcome sound, as is the drone of Allied planes, flying several miles ahead, bombing the higher terrain.

Jazz lights another cigarette while I chew a new stick of gum.

These guys did what they could for their country, I think, watching the German prisoners. Why can't you trust and treat them kindly? Now that they're prisoners, they've earned the right to return home alive when the war is over.

As I watch, Hank moves closer to the circle, a cigarette lighter in hand. "Hank," I yell. "Stay away. You're too close."

Hank turns back in annoyance. "I'm fine," he yells back. "I'm just lighting his cigarette."

Stubborn ass, I think, as I reach for my canteen. But before my hand enters my pack, Hank lets out a blood-curdling scream.

One of the Nazis has him in a headlock. The German stabs Hank again and again, yelling, "Heil Hitler, Heil Hitler."

A few shots from Jazz drops the Nazi with the knife. The others scatter, running for the open field. I open fire, running after them, side by side with Jazz. Together we drop several.

One of the Sherman tanks machine guns the rest, continuing fire until they're mutilated beyond recognition. Jazz and I count six heads in the field. The three Jazz and I shot aren't moving.

Doc tends to Hank while Coney and Country Boy corral the remaining four prisoners. "Get your Nazi ass moving or I'll crack your fucking skull!" Coney shouts.

"I want to shoot me some Krauts for stew!" yells Country Boy.

"Give those prisoners to the MP's and get back here. I don't need any more bull shit!" Sully yells at Coney and Country Boy.

As Hank struggles to breath, it's clear these moments are his last.

Hank's a good soldier. I can understand his desire to go home. He misses his country, the land of his parents and grandparents. He remembers life as a child before all the chaos caused by the Nazis. He became an American citizen, but his heart was always in Germany, just like mine would be if I was forced to leave my country for good. For a few minutes that morning, he was able to share laughs and talk about his homeland. But this is war. If you make a poor choice, you may pay with your life.

Doc's trying to stop the bleeding, but without success. He gives Hank a shot of morphine and shakes his head at Sully.

"Dammit!" Sully says, kneeling beside him.

All of us can see the multiple wounds in Hank's heart, abdomen and neck. He's bleeding profusely from all of them. Within minutes, he's gone.

Sully kneels over Hank's lifeless body and removes his dog tag and personal belongings. Then he stands up, angry. "That's why you never talk to the enemy," he yells. "They wait for you to let your guard down. Then they pounce. Got it?"

For an instant, Sully reminds me of my dad, the way he got angry with Suzanne and me when we broke a window playing. After he calmed down, he'd give us advice. "Do you understand?" he'd ask. We'd nod, but then make the same mistake again. Like my sister and I, Hank never listened to Sully's advice. But this was more serious than a broken window.

I find Coney sitting on a log. "You ok?" I ask.

He's puffing on his cigarette. "Yeah, I'm fine," he says. "Why?"

I know him well enough that he doesn't look fine to me. "Are you angry at Hank?" I ask.

Coney shakes his head in frustration. "Yes," he says. "Why didn't he listen to Sully? Damn. He'd still be alive."

"Mike," I say, "Let's face it. Hank never listened to anyone other than himself. He had a dream that if he could find someone from his childhood, that would eliminate all the pain he'd suffered because of the Nazis."

"When the hell did you get so smart?" Coney asks, reaching over and slapping me on the back. "Thanks, buddy."

My mind is racing with questions, just like Coney. I wish I had been smarter with Danny Boy. I repaid him for saving my life by leading him out of a foxhole to his death. I don't know how Sully handles the burden of leading guys into combat. Right now, two squad brothers have died under my watch.

Under the noon sun, we dig a shallow grave for Hank.

Sully tries to give us good news. "The battle last night, although costly to the squad, was important. According to headquarters, we stopped a large enemy drive heading east."

Sully looks around at us, and raises his canteen. "Here's to our fallen brothers. Let's have some rations before we move out."

We talk quietly, appreciating a few minutes of peace.

CHAPTER 16

"Arty, can you give me a hand?" Sully asks.

"Sure," I reply.

Sully kneels and spreads out a map. "Hold the map flat." I kneel beside him, holding the edges of the map down, while he traces a path with his pen.

"We talked before, Arty," Sully says. "But I want to remind you. I'm sick every time a squad brother dies or is wounded under my command. Why am I alive?"

It's the same question I've been asking myself, but Sully doesn't meet my eyes when he asks it. He's still looking down at the map.

"I know you're feeling responsible for the deaths of Lucky and Danny Boy," he tells me. "But you did nothing wrong. In fact, you helped Lucky on the ship. He was a good kid and his heart was in the right place. But he wasn't a soldier. I assigned Lucky to you because you're patient and thoughtful. The difference between Lucky and you is you learned to be brave. No one's born brave. You've learned to bury your fears.

"I watched you with Danny Boy," Sully goes on. "He was visibly scared when he first landed. I put him behind you on the road so you could watch out for him. During that first firefight you helped him focus and fire at the enemy. If you hadn't helped him then how long do you think he would've lived? When soldiers join up, you never know how they'll perform in combat. Combat is not natural. None of us are raised to kill another human being. That's what separates war from anything else in life.

"Arty," Sully says, finally looking up at me, "you have an ability to engage people and lead them. I've seen it. But like it or not, soldiers die. I'm telling you this because I'm proud of how much you've grown as a soldier. We have a long way to go on this island and I need your head in the war."

He looks back down at the map and folds it up. "Thanks for the help," he says.

I'm at a loss for words. Sully can see strengths in me that I never knew existed. He believes in my abilities and trusts me to guide others in horrible situations. It makes me feel confident but also uncomfortable.

While I'm still trying to take his encouragement in, Sully goes over to the rest of the squad. "We're combining with other squads," he tells everyone, "to flush out German and Italian units from pockets to our west. These smaller groups are left behind to cause chaos while the main enemy moves northeast. Be ready in 10 minutes at 1300 hours."

"Any news on when we'll have a break off the line?" Coney asks.

"I haven't heard anything about leaving the line," Sully says. "But word is there may be a cafeteria truck available after this mission. There are secure locations west. For now, the best I can offer is a hot meal."

Coney smiles. "That's a start."

After a couple miles of rough terrain, we approach a hilltop.

"Stay low," Sully whispers, gesturing for us to climb. "Stop short of the top."

When we reach the rise, Sully pulls out a map. "We're on this hillside," he says, pointing. "On the other side is a bridge. The bridge and surrounding areas are prime sites for enemy traps. They may be prepared to blow the bridge. Or the intersection may be a trap for trucks. I'm going to check it out. Stay here."

He crawls cautiously to the top of the hill, pokes his head over, and surveys the ground below with field binoculars. After a few minutes he descends to us again. "There's a bridge at the bottom," he tells us. "A mortar crew is one hundred yards to the left, hidden by brush. They've got a machine gun and a crew of four at the intersection with the bridge. On the road beyond the bridge, there's a truck."

Sully looks up at the sky. "The sun will be at our backs," he says. "We'll need the glare for cover. Jazz and Country Boy, find a spot to set up our machine gun. Coney, move close enough to distract the enemy machine gunners with grenades." He looks around at the rest of us. "Each of you," he says, "give grenades to Coney. Arty, position yourself to lay fire on the nest. I'm going with the others to attack the mortar crew. I'll see you all on the bridge."

Coney and I follow Jazz and Country Boy down the incline at a forty five degree angle. There's no path. We maneuver slowly, trying not to slip on loose rocks, fallen branches or gravel. We have to duck to keep from getting smacked in the face by low-hanging branches of trees. Unfortunately, none of them bear fruit. But moving through vegetation is better than moving through the bare patches of the hill, where we're totally exposed.

"Jazz, can't you move any faster?" Coney asks. "Need help with that gun?"

"Don't worry about me," Jazz jokes. "Just keep Country Boy in line. He keeps spitting in front of me."

"Guys, I see an area over here," says Jazz. "I'll set up off of this ledge and fire to the right. I'll give you five minutes to get a drop on their position and then we'll open up."

"Thanks for the warning," I say. "See you at the bridge."

A few minutes later, we've descended to within forty yards of the road.

"I'll continue," Coney whispers. "Do you have a shot?"

I give a thumbs up. I've got a clear line of sight to the machine gun nest through an opening in the trees. Once I empty a round I'll descend even further.

Coney acknowledges. Crouching, he stretches his left shoulder, winding up to toss grenades.

He's scrambled ten yards down the hill, heading for the machine gun nest when Jazz and Country Boy open up a steady *rat, tat, tat, rat, tat, tat*. I aim at the machine gun nest and fire at the spotter to the left. My first shot hits his shoulder. He falls, reaching for his rifle. My second shot misses, but my third hits his head. The gunner and ammunition assistant are blocked by trees. Flushed out by our fire, other Germans run from the bridge. I drop a couple more, then reload, moving down the hill.

Mortar shells start to land on the slope around us. Jazz and Country Boy continue to fire, as Coney begins to rain a hail of grenades around the machine gun nest. Several Germans stumble up from the other side of the road, but quickly fall to the ground, motionless, under our fire. The mortar shells are starting to zero in on Jazz and Country Boy, forcing them further down the hill.

To the left, near Coney, two Germans rush to set up another machine gun. I take aim, but my first two shots miss. Adjusting slightly, I wound one German in his left thigh, but he continues to assist, holding the ammunition belt as the gunner opens a stream of fire. My next two shots don't miss, dropping the assistant.

The gunner pushes the dead assistant away from the gun. With that motion he provides me an open target. I fire and hit him in the shoulder. As he turns in pain, a grenade lands in the nest, blowing it all to bits. Fire from Jazz and Country Boy sprays the other nest, silencing their guns.

The sporadic gunfire from beyond the bridge stills and the mortar shells cease to drop. I step cautiously onto the road, Coney at my left. When we arrive at the first nest, smoke still gently rises from the end of the gun. I push away the gunner with my rifle and his mangled body flops onto the ground. What's left of his head turns, revealing a bloody mess in place of his face. Coney prods the other two dead bodies to ensure they're dead before we move on.

Jazz and Country Boy approach from the bridge. "No explosives at the bridge," Jazz calls out. "I'm going to destroy these guns." He removes each gun on the bridge from its tripod and slams the trigger device into the blocks along the bridge.

Sully emerges from the woods, waving his left hand above his head, followed by Doc and several other infantry. "We neutralized two mortar crews, but the third one escaped into the truck," he reports. "How about you?"

"We secured the bridge and intersection with no casualties," Jazz replies. "We didn't find explosives under the bridge and there are no enemy survivors."

"Nice job," Sully says. But his expression is still serious. "Damn," he adds. "I'm worried about the escaped mortar crew. I shouldn't have let them get away. Ammo up and hydrate."

As we break out our canteens, I hear trucks approaching from behind. We slip into the brush just in time to see the trucks are marked with the familiar large black star of the American Army. As they pass, several men from the convoy acknowledge us. We wave back and head out on the road again, walking towards the northwest.

"Hey, hop in," a driver yells. "I'm heading in your direction."

Sully's face lights up as he recognizes the driver. "Clarence!" he shouts. "Get in, guys," he tells us. "I'll ride shotgun."

We climb in the back, sitting six on each side, across from each other. This is an unexpected gift. Any infantryman will tell you, after all the time we spend on our feet, riding is the only way to go. I chew a fresh piece of gum. Coney lights Jazz's cigarette and they both sit back, contented. Doc inventories his med pack while Country Boy tries to nap. A few minutes later, Jazz begins whistling his familiar song.

It's better than walking, but the truck is not the lap of luxury. The wooden seats are hard and I could swear there's not one shock absorber. "Damn," says Coney, as the truck takes a series of harsh jolts. "What are we riding over—foxholes?" Another stretch of road is so bad that we actually smack our heads together.

After fifteen minutes the truck stops. We climb out into an open field, where two cafeteria trucks are stationed.

Sully bangs on the hood as he hops out of the shotgun seat. "Thanks for the lift, Clarence."

As the truck pulls out, Sully joins us, all smiles. "Good to see Clarence," he says. "He was the convoy driver I initiated into the infantry a few days back." Then he turns towards the field. "Time to eat!"

"Arty, what's that smell?" Coney jokes, and plugs his nose. "Could that be real food?"

"Smells like spaghetti and meatballs!" says Jazz.

"I hope you're right!" I say happily. "Hmm… spaghetti, meatballs and thick Italian bread."

"Jazz is right," Coney replies. "We're having spaghetti, meatballs, bread and limeade."

For the past nine days, since we boarded the vessel in North Africa, we've been eating rations and scrounging anything we can find. A spaghetti and meatball dinner is long overdue.

CHAPTER 17

The two trucks are parked under shade trees to the left of the road. A white barn stands on the opposite side of the field. The remains of a white fence run the length of the field, straight ahead. This would be a perfect place for a pick-up baseball game.

"Hey Coney," I say. "After we eat, want to throw?"

"You got it, sport," Coney says. "I was beginning to think I wouldn't be using my glove on this island. This will be the third continent we'll play ball on! I need to stretch my shoulder." In line for the food, he begins to stretch. The guys around him duck to keep from getting smacked in the face.

After filling our plates, we assemble in a circle of six, still close enough to the trucks to go back for seconds.

"Y'all," Country Boy says with a laugh, "I can't wait to walk into the Rockfish Pub. The owner will take one look at me in my uniform and I'll drink on the house all night long with my own spittoon."

"Yep," says Jazz, "In Nassau, I won't have to buy a beer for five years. All I'll need to do is tell war stories."

"How about you, Sully?" Coney asks.

Sully raises his eyebrows, with a faint smile. "After several plates of my mother's sausage," he says, "meatballs, eggplant, homemade bread, I'll walk to the American House and order a mug of Rheingold. Friends of my father and other veterans of The Great War will ask questions. When I tell them what we've been through, they'll line up the bar with frosty mugs." He chuckles. "I'm sure they'll tell me how much easier this war was," he adds with a chuckle.

"Sounds like my dad and his friends," I say.

"How about you, Arty?" Coney asks.

"I'll wear my uniform and polished boots to the horse track and get pitchers of free beer and racing tips," I say. "I'll have to buy a second wallet with all the money I'll win! Every night after the races, I'll walk down Broadway drinking at all the pubs—on the house. Doc," I say, turning to him, "What are your plans?"

Doc Ito sets down his plate. "I'll grab my board and ride the waves," he says, holding out his arms and bobbing around. "Then, at night, we'll have a campfire on the beach and cook fish and eat pineapple and papaya, washing it all down with spiked punch. Before the music and dancing starts I'll raise a glass to all of those I couldn't save." He seems to wince a bit, then changes the subject. "Coney, can you stop chewing long enough to tell us your plans?" Doc asks.

Coney doesn't stop chewing. Mouth full, he announces, "I'll take a train from Edison to the Bronx. I'll walk into Yankee Stadium for a tryout. Then I'll put on my uniform and get free pie and beer at my favorite pizza parlor. I'll tell stories about the bravery of the squad." Coney raises his cup. "Here's to Sully's Squad!"

"Thanks, Coney," Sully says, raising his own cup. "Here's to Lucky, Marty, Romeo, Danny Boy, Hank and Willy. A fast recovery to Wolcott and Kelly."

When I finish my last bite of bread, I set my plate and cup on the grass. For the first time in days, my stomach is full. "Coney," I say, "I may need a few minutes to digest before I catch you."

"No problem," Coney says, standing up to head back to the grub line. "I'm not done eating yet, anyway."

The break from battle gives me the time to present Sully with Danny Boy's personal letters. When I sit back down, I notice that a letter has fallen out of my own pack. It's addressed to me. Ah, I think, I forgot about the second letter from mail call. I bet it's from Suzanne.

A newspaper clipping drops out of the envelope. It's from *The Rochester Democrat and Chronicle*, and it's dated September 18, 1919. I unfold the flimsy paper and begin to read.

> *"The sun broke through the mist of yesterday's cool, crisp morning. Neighborhood residents awoke to activity in the modest white ranch on Mt. Read Boulevard. Arthur Flaherty, another of Rochester's Gold Stars, has come home from battle. Members of the Veterans of Foreign Wars and American Legion paid homage to the fallen brother. The Blue star that hung in the window is now replaced with Gold. Ladies from the Veterans Auxiliary watch silently from the sidewalk. A flag-draped casket rested in the front parlor. Neighbors such as Mrs. Anita Ryan and Mrs. Antoinette Geneteri stood on the front porches of their houses across the street, paying homage. Each wiped their eyes with handkerchiefs, mumbling and blessing themselves as they bowed their heads, clear memories of*

Arthur playing baseball in his front yard still etched in their minds.

The porch door opened, allowing passersby a glimpse of the red and white stripes draped over the casket. "Attention!" yelled John Murtaugh of the veteran's detail. The church bell from a block away began to ring intermittently. Corporal Murtaugh accompanied the remains, assisting the pallbearers in loading the casket onto a horse drawn carriage. He then led the procession to the church.

Children on the boulevard stopped playing and ran to their porches to stand with their fathers. The Mt. Read general and hardware stores closed. Cars pulled off the busy boulevard, turning off their engines out of respect.

The only sounds were chirping birds and the hooves of horses following the squeaking of wagon wheels.

Gold star mothers held onto each other, remembering the days their sons came home. Arthur's mother, Sarah Flaherty, walked in cadence with her husband, Aiden, behind the casket. At times she laid her head on his shoulder while he wiped away tears from his eyes. Arthur's younger sisters—at the tender ages of 14, 12 and 8—walked hand in hand close behind their parents. As the family arrived at the church, the procession entered for an Irish Catholic mass and liturgy with Father William O'Connor presiding.

After a few minutes, the procession arrived at the family plot, where Arthur was to be buried next to his grandparents and an older brother

*who died in infancy. The silence was broken by
birds singing a tribute, as if they were feathered
angels. At the command of the local Veterans of
Foreign War commander Lawrence Parker, the
clicking of the rifles followed by gunshots scared
them off. The echo of twenty-one shots bounced off
the surrounding trees.*

*A bugler standing on a hill overlooking the
site began "Taps." As any veteran will attest,
"Taps" tugs at the heart and brings tears to the
eyes. The flag was gently lifted and folded by
Corporal Murtaugh. His white gloves reflected
the sun peeking through the trees. He handed the
flag to Mrs. Flaherty. They shook hands and Mrs.
Flaherty returned to her chair, weeping while
pressing the flag tight to her chest.*

*As a Great War veteran, I remember falling
asleep on the base each night to the beautiful sound
of "Taps." As I report this story, I salute the memory
of my fallen comrade. Welcome home, Arthur
Flaherty. May your body and soul rest in peace."*

I fold the newspaper clipping and wipe my own eyes,
then check to see if anyone noticed my tears. They're all
busy napping or reading. I can't stop thinking how hard
it must have been on his family after he died. Then I
notice a second piece of paper in the envelope, a letter
in my Dad's handwriting. *Arthur,* it begins:

*By the time you get this you'll have seen combat.
I want you to read about my friend Arthur. He
was a brave soldier. We fought in many battles and
spent nights talking to each other about our dreams.*

He was a couple of years older than me. Everyone was older than me. I want you to know that he saved my life. We were under heavy shelling and he pushed me out of the way of a shell that landed in our foxhole. When it exploded, he took the hit and shielded me. He didn't have to do that, but he did. I didn't get the chance to say thank you. Daily I have this guilt that I'm alive and he's not. Why did he do that? Why wasn't I killed instead?

He knew I feared hand-to-hand fighting. One night he stabbed a German who jumped me. I can still see that German's face. I was hoping I could return the favor and save him but that opportunity never came.

Your mom doesn't know about him. I've never told anyone but you. I told his parents he was very brave, but I couldn't bring myself to tell them what he did and how he died. Years later, when your mom was pregnant with you, she asked: "Do you want a junior?" I told her that I don't deserve one. I want to name our son Arthur. (She was happy because she also liked the name.) Naming you after Arthur was an important way for me to thank the man who saved my life.

I learned later from someone much smarter than me that courage is doing what you're afraid to do. It's not easy, but I struggle every day knowing I wasn't given another chance to face my fears. At military funerals, I've presented flags to family members of all backgrounds. I'll never forget the looks on their faces as they cried and hugged that flag as if it represented their lost loved ones. That's *why I've always hung a flag on our front porch: to honor those young men and their families.*

Son, I want you to come home safe and live a great life and be proud of how you served your country in her time of need. Just remember that unless you've been in combat you will never be able to explain to anyone about the experience. I want you to know that I'll always be here if you want to talk. I'm hoping this isn't too much for you. Maybe I should have told you sooner. But a story like this is hard for me to tell to those I love.

Love, Dad

I finish the letter but continue to stare at the page, stunned by my Dad's vulnerability and by the story of Arthur. My namesake.

"You ok?" Sully asks, catching me wipe my eyes.

I take a deep breath and wipe my nose on my sleeve. Instead of responding, I hand him the article. He reads them both, the article and the letter.

Then he looks down at me. "Arty," he says, "to know what your dad is thinking deep down is a gift. My dad died of a heart attack when I was twelve. There's so much I would've liked to ask, but I'll never have the chance. Your namesake sounds like one hell of a soldier. You should be proud. You're representing his name well. You're one hell of a soldier, too."

Sully pats me on the shoulder and walks away. I fold the newspaper clipping and then fold the letter around it. I place them securely in my chest pocket, trying to get used to a new feeling: for the first time, I understand my father. Though we're separated by continents and oceans, I feel closer to him than ever before. There is peace in that.

The comforting feeling doesn't last long. In a flash, my surge of admiration and love for my father is replaced by the will to survive. Screams ring out through the field: "Incoming! Incoming!"

The chorus of shells screams from beyond the white fence as soldiers scramble for safety all over the field around the cafeteria trucks.

I grab my pack and rifle and race for cover behind the barn along with Jazz and Country Boy, as mortar shells explode at our heels. *The mortar team Sully hadn't been able to find! They've found us.*

I bury my head between my hands as mortar shells continue to drop onto the field. Coney and I had hoped to make it into a baseball diamond. Now it was just another piece of land destroyed by war.

The barrage appears to stop. I slowly lift my head. One of the cafeteria trucks is on fire, and then *kaboom*—a secondary explosion blows off the wheels. I bury my head again. I glance over to Jazz and Country Boy, still lying low and assessing the scene. The smell of burning fuel hangs over the field. *Those poor cooks never had a chance*, I think. *They didn't deserve this death, and neither did the poor guys standing in line for a well-earned meal.*

I rise slowly, swiveling my head defensively, on guard for the next strike as I venture back to the field. As the smoke dissipates, I look to where we were all sitting. Is someone lying face down? I begin to run. The body's exposed left side is covered in blood. I roll him over: It's Sully.

CHAPTER 18

Sully tries to stand, pushing himself up on his right arm. His eyes race back and forth as he tries to yell: "C'mon, let's get those krauts. I knew they'd find us. I need too…" he falls back, on the border of unconsciousness.

I hold Sully's head and stare into his anxious eyes: "Sully, you need to focus. You're wounded. Stay with me."

I turn, yelling "Doc, Doc, over here!" Facing Sully again, I say through gritted teeth: "We'll find those bastards!"

Doc is suddenly kneeling next to me. "He's breathing," I say. "And his wounds are on the left side."

"Thanks, Arty," Doc says, breaking out his kit. "I have it. Go find a jeep. I'll wrap and medicate him." Turning back to Sully while he works, Doc adds: "Don't you worry—you'll be back in this war in no time."

I grab my pack and sprint to the road. Wounded are being helped into an ambulance truck, but the vehicle pulls out before I can reach it. I turn to the road and wave down a jeep speeding towards me from around a bend. A man jumps out of the passenger side. "Sir," I say urgently, "I need to borrow your jeep—my Sargent is wounded."

He turns to his driver: "Help him," he directs, then sprints towards the field.

The driver follows me back to Sully, and I don't think he can tell how scared and distraught I am inside. Ever since basic training, Sully has been the constant—the cornerstone I've counted on. Now he's a bloody pulp, wavering in and out of consciousness as Doc works to keep him alive.

Sully lifts himself up and grabs my hand. He looks me in the eyes, which are full of pain, but he still manages to whisper, "Remember, keep your cool and you'll do well. See you soon."

"C'mon, Arty," Coney yells, running up. "We're joining another squad to find those motherfuckers."

Sully had been afraid the escaped mortar crew would cause us harm, and they did. During that short barrage, six soldiers were killed, including army cooks. And several were wounded like Sully.

For the first time since landing, we're directly following Lieutenant Cook.

He lays out a plan for us, pointing to a map. "We're estimating that crew was two hundred yards from the field," he tells us. "I need you," he goes on, nodding at Coney, Jazz, Country Boy, and me, "to go through those fields. They're still here. We need to flush them out.

"A half mile up the road we'll infiltrate this wooded area," he says, indicating a brown region on the map. "The rest of you join me on the road as a target. Once they fire at us we'll attack from the right flank and call in artillery.

"There may be snipers and machine guns placed ahead of the mortars," the lieutenant warns, "so be alert. We'll meet back here after we neutralize them."

We break off into the field, and within minutes, mortar shells begin to land close to the road. The Lieutenant was right that the escaped mortar team wouldn't be able to resist a target.

But our little group is maneuvering across open land, trying to get a read on where those mortars are coming from. "Follow me," yells Jazz. "There's an open area ahead, perfect for mortars."

Several hundred yards, Jazz commands, "We'll set up here. Arty and Coney, flank them from behind and chase them to the open field. We'll mow the fuckers down when they run ahead."

Coney and I hide beyond a tree line about fifty yards to the left of Jazz and Country Boy, hoping we've run parallel to the position of the mortar crew. So far, no sign of snipers and machine guns. But at least we know we're behind them now.

"Get down, Coney," I whisper. "I can hear a German truck idling through trees. You get close enough to throw grenades at the crew. I'll take care of the enemy in the truck."

"Yes sir, Arty," Coney says. It's a joke, but he nods to acknowledge my orders.

The sound of mortar projectiles covers the noise of my own movement as I approach the idling truck. My heart pounds through my chest as I get close enough to look inside. I have a sick feeling that the truck is not empty.

The truck is camouflaged light brown, with swastikas on the front doors and mirrors on either side. I crouch and scan the area below the passenger side of the truck. As I do, explosions from Coney's grenades begin to go off, punctuating the blast of mortar shells.

With my rifle I slowly lift the cloth covering the back of the truck. Crates full of ammunition labeled *mortelschalen* in large black letters are piled inside. Even with my ignorance of languages, I can figure out this means mortars.

"Ahh!" A large figure jumps from behind the crates and lands on me, knocking me back onto the ground. I try jumping up but he's on top, punching and kicking.

I duck my head and roll to either side looking for my rifle as he rains down blows on me, yelling "Amerikanisch, Amerikanisch." When I can't find my rifle, I remember what I did with the last German who attacked me. I grab hands full of gravel and throw them right into his face. But the glare through the trees prevents me from getting a clear look at him.

Suddenly, he's got a knife. I roll away as he lunges at me. He stabs the ground, which allows me the chance to pull my own knife out and get to my feet. My breathing is heavy and blood trickles from my nose into my mouth. I spit it out, assessing my adversary as we circle each other. His uniform is fit very tight around his mid-section; he has no neck and outweighs me by at least 50 pounds. The Afrika Korp insignia on his shoulder indicates he could be a part of the Kesselring division. He smiles as he taunts me in broken English. "You're nothing but a puny boy. Why do Amerikanisch fight with such little boys? Come here so I can kill you!" Behind us is nothing but explosions and gunfire. I'm on my own. There's no Sully or Coney to help. I have to handle this situation.

"Afrika Korp!" I say. "The last time I saw a patch like that was on dead Nazis in North Africa. Sorry Amerikanisch boys had to kill so many of your friends. If I was you I'd remove that patch since you're not in North Africa anymore, asshole. This is Sicily."

His face grows angrier. He must understand some English. He tosses a fistful of gravel and rocks at me.

"Nice try," I say, dodging. "I can tell you never played a sport. Your throwing arm is weak." As I tease him, I hear Sully's voice in my head: *keep cool and you'll do well.*

"You'll have to do better than that if you want to kill me, Adolf," I say. "Did you hear that machine gun? My squad has been taking down everyone you know. Soon you'll be alone to fight against twenty Amerikanisch. Why don't you just drop the knife and I'll take you prisoner."

By the way he looks around, I can see I'm getting to him. I just have to become more creative. Out of the corner of my eye I see my rifle on the ground a few yards away. I crouch, pretending my stomach is hurting.

Keep your cool, keep your cool.

I need to keep fueling his rage. I stand but again fake pain and drop to my knees. He's still taking feints at me with his knife but now he's hesitating.

Why is he hesitating? I wonder. *And why doesn't he have a rifle? Did he jump out of the truck without it? Why wouldn't he grab it? Is he a truck driver, not experienced infantry?*

The heat's starting to affect him now, too. He wipes his eyes. I use the moment of distraction to drop to the ground and roll towards my rifle. I get my hands on it while he's still trying to figure out what's going on, then I jump up and charge him. When I knock him in the chest with the rifle butt, he falls back, hitting his head on the ground. He struggles up and lunges at me yet again. I whack his lower leg with my rifle, and hear bone crack as he drops.

"Ah, Scheisse," he screams. He's trying to stand, but he can't. "I'll kill you!"

I aim at his head. "Give up," I say evenly, "or I'll blow your fucking head off!"

He begins to kneel, knife still in his hand, but the pain from his leg causes him to fall. I circle him, attaching the bayonet to my rifle as he pivots on his knees.

The thought of just stepping back and shooting him in the head keeps running through my mind. *Arthur,* something says, *he's a no good Nazi scum. Just kill him before he kills you.* But, something else tells me to stand up and fight, not murder him.

"Raise your arms," I yell. "Raise your arms and surrender!"

Even on his knees, he continues to lunge at me. "I'll kill you, I'll kill you," he yells. I knock the knife out of his hand with the bayonet, slicing his palm. His hand begins to bleed. "Ah Gott Verdammt," he yells. Now he's on all fours, looking down.

Within me, the battle continues. *Shoot this Nazi bastard. You've seen what they did to your friends and civilians.* Instead, I discharge orders: "Raise your arms. Raise your arms and surrender!" I continue yelling.

He stays down on all fours, but then I see him grab for something under his shirt. I stab him in his shoulder and recoil. He rolls on his back, holding his shoulder. With his other hand he continues to reach for something under his belt.

He would've shot you in the head if he had the chance, that inner voice says. *Why are you keeping this shithead alive?*

But I don't want to live my life knowing I committed outright murder.

I knock him in the head with the butt of my rifle. As he recoils, a German grenade drops to the ground near him.

"Fuck!" I jump away with every muscle in my body, hitting the ground just as the grenade goes off. A second, larger explosion engulfs the truck in flames. I hug the ground like a worm trying to burrow into it. The air feels like a furnace. Hot objects rain down around me.

After what seems like an eternity, I lift my head. In front of the burning truck I see a uniformed body on fire.

I pound the ground with my fist. "That's for Sully and me, damn it!" The emotion of the moment overcomes me. I'm still alive, and I defeated the German. I didn't let my inner conflict steer me wrong. I kept Sully's reminder to stay calm in the forefront of my mind.

I remove my helmet, take a drink from my canteen, and dump water on my head. Then I start walking towards the meeting point.

"Hey, Arty!" Coney emerges from a stand of trees. "Damn," he says, when he gets a look at me. "You're a mess. You ok?"

"I'm fine," I tell him. "I fought a German guarding the ammo truck. Dumb ass wouldn't surrender, but now he's dead. How did you guys make out?"

"We neutralized the mortars. All those Nazis who wounded Sully are dead," Coney replies. I can see the pride of accomplishment in his expression. "We're going to the mobile hospital tomorrow morning in Mazzarino," he continues. "Lieutenant Cook said we deserve a few hours off the line to visit Sully and give him the news."

"Great!" I reply. "I can't wait to see Sully."

I'm also happy I'll be able to see Angelina.

CHAPTER 19

"Here you go, boys," the driver says as we come to an abrupt stop in front of the hospital tent. Coney, Jazz, Country Boy and I hop out. The hospital has been relocated from inside the church in town to the outskirts of Mazzarino.

"Arty," Coney says. "There's the castle!"

I smile as I remember our mission to clear the castle, and what we'd found there. I'm glad there's plenty of room for the hospital in the field next door.

The hospital is full of activity, with nurses wheeling patients towards surgery and hooking up IVs. We find Sully sitting up in bed. His left arm and shoulder are bandaged, but he appears otherwise unscathed.

"Sully," Jazz says with a grin. "You look like you're on vacation."

"Glad to see you, brother," Sully says, extending his right hand. "I'm doing okay. They just removed the IV and I had a good sleep. How about you?"

"Doing well," Jazz says. "Lieutenant Cook sent us. We only have a few hours, but he wanted us to tell you personally that the mortar crew is neutralized."

"I heard a number of guys were killed and wounded," Sully says, dejectedly. "I should've..."

"Sully, you can't blame yourself," Jazz interrupts

sternly. "Shit happens in war. C'mon, you've saved all of us multiple times since North Africa."

A glob of brown spit lands near my boot. "Ah, Country Boy's here." I say.

Country Boy says, "Ya'll, I got a surprise in my pack." He slowly reveals a can of beer.

"What're you doing? I can't drink in here," Sully whispers.

"Sully you're fine. After all they just removed your IV," Jazz jokes. He takes a quick look around, then bends over and coughs, covering the sound of the beer can opening. Then he hands it over. "Here, Sully," he says. "A prelude to Messina."

"Where's Doc?" I ask.

As if on cue, Doc comes up, pushing an empty wheelchair. He takes one look at the beer can, then points at the door. "Outside."

With effort and a hand from the nurse, Sully moves himself from the bed to the wheelchair. Then we follow Doc as he pushes Sully out through a side door, overlooking the castle.

In the fresh air, Jazz opens his pack again, this time pulling out a bottle of wine.

"Where'd you get that?" Doc asks.

"I have my ways," Jazz replies slyly, yanking out the cork. He takes a swig and passes the bottle to Country Boy, who does the same before handing it to me for a turn.

Sully raises the can to his lips. "This beer tastes like freedom." He shakes his head, staring thoughtfully into the middle distance. "I'm privileged to be your Sargent."

"To Sully's Squad!" says Jazz.

"Cheers!" we shout in chorus.

As the guys begin to swap stories, I decide to sneak away. We've only got three hours before we're supposed to be back on the line, and I need to find Angelina.

For the first time in over a week, I walk down a road without keeping an alert for snipers, shells or landmines. I have a new definition of freedom: not worrying that the next step you take may be your last.

Mazzarino is much busier now than before. Trucks and jeeps pass by full of soldiers and supplies. Townspeople fill the sidewalks, walking briskly and conversing. Planted pots replace the white sheets that I'd seen hanging from windows days before. Stores are open and customers sit at tables outside several restaurants, enjoying lunch and carrying on lively conversations. Townspeople greet me with a smile or nod. Men and kids of all ages offer me salutes. Ladies lean over their balconies, smiling, and wave as I pass. A feeling of pride comes over me. My squad brothers and I helped this town reclaim their lives.

Approaching the church, I see children playing soccer in the front. The mobile hospital tents are gone, but blood stains on the ground remain as evidence of the wounded men who were cared for here.

I remove my helmet and open the church door. The same musty air greets me as I walk up the aisle to one of the front pews, where I remove my pack, set my rifle down, and sit. I find myself staring ahead, and enjoying the quiet. The rainbow shining on the altar is so beautiful I leave the pew to get a closer look. I stand before the altar, staring at a flickering candle flame. The black smoke rises from it as I quickly run my index finger in and out of the flame—one of the I-dare-you games I used to play with my sister Suzanne.

Several statues surround the communion table. The only one I recognize is the cross. I pull my rosary over my head and look at the cross. Until now, I'd never noticed that it was a crucifix, or looked closely at the detailed craftsmanship.

"May I help you?" a woman says. She's wearing black and walking towards me. Her head is completely covered, leaving only her face visible.

"Yes, ma'am," I say with a bow. "I'm looking for Angelina."

She nods and smiles. "Are you Arthur?"

"Yes," I answer, giving her a confused look.

"Angelina talks about how nice you've been," she tells me. "We pray for you daily." Her gaze drifts to the rosary in my hands. "You're holding a rosary," she says. "Do you say the rosary?"

"No ma'am," I confess. "Angelina gave it to me. I wear it around my neck."

"Well that's wonderful, Arthur," she says with a smile. "The Lord will always be close to you."

"Sister," I tell her, "I'm in combat. He's not there. At least I hope he's not. Combat is not a nice place."

"Arthur," she says, nodding, "I can only imagine how difficult it is to be soldier. God knows you didn't start the war and that you're a loving boy in a challenging situation. I'll find Angelina," she says, walking away. "God bless you, Arthur."

I always find myself confused with religion, and usually say the wrong things. As I'm standing there, thinking about the conversation, a familiar soft voice interrupts my thoughts.

"Arthur, I'm so happy to see you." Angelina is walking down the aisle of the church towards me, smiling.

She greets me with a hug, the rosary beads still dangling from my hands. I return the hug and a feeling of warmth energizes my body.

"I'm sorry," I say as I back away. "I hope I didn't get dirt from my uniform on you."

Like the townspeople, Angelina seems more alive, more talkative. "I'm fine, Arthur," she says, excitement in her voice. "I'm so happy the Germans are out of here and retreating north. Soon my brother and I will reunite with my parents. Thank you. You and all the brave soldiers who've given so much for us."

I nod, realizing that she's right. I've seen what my squad alone has sacrificed. However, I can't think of anything else to say besides, "Can I have another hug, for them?"

She smiles. "I've got something better," she says, then comes closer and kisses me on the lips. My legs go weak.

"We're in church," I whisper.

She smiles and lowers her head, "I'm sorry," she says. "For the first time in years, I see an end to this horrific war and my life returning to back to me. I just want to show my appreciation to a young man who has helped make this happen."

I hold her hand, smiling myself. "I'm perfectly happy to receive your kisses."

She giggles. "The children are outside with the others. Mother Superior told me you're here."

"That was Mother Superior? She's very nice. Please thank everyone for praying for me."

"Prego," she responds with a wink. *You're welcome.*

Then she squeezes my hand. "I have a surprise for you. Let's go. We have to be quick. I need to be back for dinner," she tells me. We rush out of the church.

"Where are we going?" I ask.

She smiles. "You'll see. Just keep up with me, soldier, and we can make it in 20 minutes."

I'm carrying all my gear, and my pack is heavy, but I'm not complaining. Time with Angelina is precious. I forget about my eighty pound pack and rifle as I try to keep up, dodging tree branches like bullets. The terrain is flat and I can see the shoreline ahead. Angelina looks back and smiles as she leads the way. She continues to amaze me with her kindness and toughness. I have a strange feeling inside when I think of her or say her name.

We finally reach a road with several small homes, and her pace slackens. Trees along the way provide shade and offer good spots to store fishing boats.

"Stay here," she says, stopping at a spot a little way down the road. "I'll be back."

I sit on a large rock and stare into the sea as she goes into one of the houses. I enjoy watching the grace and beauty of seafaring birds flying in and over the water. The rhythmic sound of ocean waves washing on shore. Deep breaths of the cool salty air refresh me.

The sound of a snapping twig startles me. I dive

behind the rock and reach for my rifle. Then, peaking over the rock, I spot Angelina.

"What are you doing on the ground?" she asks.

A woman and two toddlers accompany her.

I stand up, embarrassed, but Angelina smiles. "Arthur," she says. "I'd like to introduce you to Gabriele and her two children, Antonio and Assunta."

I extend my hand to Gabriele. The top of her head comes to just above Angelina's shoulder. Her tan skin shows the impact of hard work in the sun. She's barefoot, dressed in a light colored top and brown skirt. Her black hair is tied back and her smile could light up a room. Her children are adorable. Antonio wears a sleeveless white T-shirt and brown shorts. Assunta curtseys, holding the sides of her brown dress, two white bows shining in her black curly hair.

"Very nice to meet you," I tell Gabriele, smiling. "Your children are beautiful." She looks at Angelina, who interprets.

"Grazie, grazie," Gabriele says in response to my compliment, drawing her children close.

"Prego," I say, reaching into my pack. "Would you like chocolate?" I kneel on one knee in front of the children, holding out two bars of chocolate.

They look at their mother, who smiles.

"Si!" they chorus. "Cioccolato!" Four little hands reach for the bars. God only knows how long it's been since they've tasted something sweet.

But they still remember to say "Grazie" as they rip open the wrappers. The smiles on each of their faces help to make everything I've been through worthwhile. *Can I please have the memory of their happy faces,* I think, *instead of the horrors I've seen?*

But I can see the sun sinking down the sky, and I know we don't have much time to stay here before we have to get back. "Angelina, this is very nice but why am I here?" I ask.

"Look out in the water. Willy's out at sea," Angelina replies, pointing. "Gabriele says Willy is very nice. He's strong and a hard worker. After just a couple of days, he already works well with the other fisherman."

"Yes," I say, laughing. "He's strong as a bull."

She smiles. "He's working as a fisherman to help provide for Gabriele and her family. The children lost their father a year ago. So he's staying for now until he decides what he wants to do. Maybe he will grow to love it and will never leave."

Angelina turns to Gabriele and speaks softly.

"Si," Gabriele replies, and points down the beach. We thank them and walk in the direction she pointed.

The peaceful sound of the waves is even more soothing down on the beach. I reach for Angelina's hand and her soft fingers twine with mine.

"Thank you for bringing me here," I say. She places her head on my shoulder. Another strange feeling comes over me.

I shield my eyes from the sun's glare off of the greenish blue water and white sand. Fifty yards out in the water, three men are pulling in a net full of catch.

"Gabriele says he's on that boat," Angelina tells me.

I cover my eyes from the glare and recognize his stocky frame among the smaller and thinner Sicilian fishermen. I want to yell out, but I think wiser of it. I turn back and thank Gabriele, handing a couple more chocolate bars to Antonio and Assunta, whose faces are now smeared with the melting delicacy.

"Angelina," I say, "thank you for bringing me to see Willy."

The walk back is slower, our hands linked together all the way. When we arrive back in town, the sun is just above the tree line. "I need to get back to the hospital," I tell her, "and see Sully and the guys."

"Willy spoke highly of Sully," Angelina says with a smile. "He says you're in good hands, being a member of Sully's Squad."

I laugh and embrace her. "That's true."

"He also spoke very highly of you," she continues. "You are brave in battle and a marksman with your shot." She stops and smiles, looking into my eyes, "he also thought you looked very young for your age."

Hmm, I am surprised that Willy considered me a marksman and brave in battle. Always seemed like he was off in his own thoughts and oblivious to what others were doing.

"Wait right there," she says, starting into the church. "I have something before you go."

It's mid-afternoon, and she returns with a late lunch. Sitting in the garden, I quickly enjoy Italian bread, fresh olives and peaches. She pours me several cups of cold water and sneaks one of red wine. I don't want this afternoon to end, but after a few more minutes, I kiss her hand. "I can't remember having this much fun," I tell her. "I'll be back. I want to see you again."

"I had a wonderful time," she says, pressing a package of Italian bread, olives and peaches into my hands. "And yes, I'll see you again."

I bend over to kiss her cheek, put my helmet on and slide my rifle over my right shoulder. When I've gone a few steps down the street, I turn back and wave. "Arty," she calls. "I'll see you in Messina!"

CHAPTER 20

Walking back to the hospital, I find myself oblivious to the sights and sounds of the streets. My mind is filled with memories of the day, and Angelina's last words to me. See me in Messina. What did that mean?

I have the same confusing feelings I had the last time I had to leave Angelina behind. Spending time with her made me happier than anything. I should just be glad we had a few more hours together. But now I miss her. Could this be what love is like?

The squad is still standing around outside the hospital when I return and see an empty beer can and two empty bottles of wine in a nearby bucket.

"Arty," Coney says. "You missed the party. We've been wondering when you'd return. We just ran out of wine. What do you have in the bag?"

Coney reaches into the bag of food Angelina gave me and rips off a piece of bread, then hands the rest to Sully. Coney alternates bites of peach with bites of fresh bread. "Hmmm," he mumbles as crumbs fall out of his mouth. "This is amazing."

Pretty soon everyone in the squad has had a bit of something from the package. The bag is empty within minutes.

"Arty," Sully says, wiping his mouth, "thanks for bringing the food."

Maybe it's the booze that makes him ask the next question. "How the hell old are you?"

My father had prepared me to answer this question. I reply with a straight face. "I'm nineteen," I tell him. "I enlisted after graduating from High School last year."

"Sorry," Sully says with a smile. "You look so young for your age. I feel like an old man of twenty-one when I'm around you."

"Time to get back to the war, fellas," Jazz reminds us. "Sully, you've trained us well. Take care of yourself. We'll see you when you return."

"Thanks, guys," Sully says. "I want you to know that I've sent home the personal belongings of the men we lost from this squad. And, Arty," he says, meeting my eyes, "I've also sent Mel's."

"Thank you," I say. "I'm glad his family will have something to remember him."

Sully wipes something from his eye. "Jazz," he orders, "come here." They shake hands and hug. Then Sully hugs each of us as we leave. I can see the pain it causes him to stay behind while his squad moves out.

"Feels kind of weird leaving without Sully," Coney says, stretching his left shoulder as if the familiar motion gives him some kind of comfort.

"He'll be back and better than ever," Country Boy says, spitting juice on the gravel street.

Jazz stops whistling long enough to agree. "Yeah," he says. "Sully will be back for the stretch run to Messina."

"Wait up!" Doc Ito yells as we start off down the road, running to catch up with us. "I just talked with the Lieutenant on the radio. We have to meet six re-placements at the entrance of town."

"Well," Coney replies, "better late than never. I hope these guys have had combat experience."

I turn and face everyone. "We're Sully's Squad," I say. "We'll train them to be the best."

Sully has trained each of us for combat. And whether he knew it or not, he also trained us for any other life challenges we may face—through him we've learned the importance of heeding wisdom, persevering, working hard, and looking out for those we love. For the next week or so we'll be on our own. But because of his guidance and encouragement, I feel confident returning to combat.

I look forward to the end of this island battle. I'll be with Angelina again and someday go home to see my family and friends. I can't wait to sit in my back-yard with my father and share our war experiences. How ironic that I had to deceive my parents to enlist in order to find a common bond with my father: be-ing a soldier.

"Hey Arty," Coney yells. "Stop dreaming and get in the truck!"

★ ★ ★

Be on the lookout for more
adventures with Sully's Squad!

ABOUT THE AUTHOR

I reside in upstate New York as a married father of three adult children. I realized after my last child was close to graduating from college that I needed to find a hobby. Although, no formal training on creative writing, I enjoy story-telling and developing historical stories of a period in history which impacts each of us, World War II. The men and women of that generation were truly special. Their sacrifice must remain historically documented for future generations to understand. *Sully's Squad* is the first in a series of accounts that I hope you enjoy. A portion of the proceeds will be contributed to organizations who support those and their families suffering from the impacts of war. I look forward to hearing from you. Please let me know about your reading experience, with *Sully's Squad,* at authwils11@gmail.com